STIFF

Stories by
Steve Hughes

WAYNE STATE UNIVERSITY PRESS
DETROIT

Made in Michigan Writers Series

General Editors

Michael Delp, Interlochen Center for the Arts

M. L. Liebler, Wayne State University

© 2018 by Steve Hughes. Published by Wayne State University Press, Detroit, Michigan 48201. All rights reserved. No part of this book may be reproduced without formal permission. Manufactured in the United States of America.

ISBN 978-0-8143-4588-7 (paperback); ISBN 978-0-8143-4589-4 (ebook)

Library of Congress Control Number: 2018948388

michigan
council for
&arts
cultural
affairs

Publication of this book was made possible by a generous gift from The Meijer Foundation. This work is supported in part by an award from the Michigan Council for Arts and Cultural Affairs.

The stories in this collection were read aloud in various forms at the Good Tyme Writers Buffet, a literary series Hughes started in 2011 and continues to run at the Public Pool Art Space in Hamtramck, MI.

Wayne State University Press
Leonard N. Simons Building
4809 Woodward Avenue
Detroit, Michigan 48201–1309

Visit us online at wsupress.wayne.edu

For Hamtramck, For Detroit

Honey gotta help me please

Somebody gotta save my soul

Baby, detonate for me . . . Oh

 —James Osterberg, "Search and Destroy"

CONTENTS

Lucky Fucking Day

I was sitting in Cindy's kitchen when she said she wasn't comfortable with the shape of my head. She didn't like the woody little stub that grew out of its center and stuck up over the dome of my skull. She didn't like my orange, ruddy complexion. She didn't like it that the holes for my eyes were shrinking and relaxing. I explained that's just what they do. And it's actually more comfortable that way. I looked at myself in the mirror. The old carving job that my wife had done, months back, was growing shut.

I didn't decide to have a head like this. I didn't make it myself any more than I named myself. I didn't have anything to do with it. Still, I knew that Cindy was right. I needed my stalk trimmed and shaped. I needed my features sharpened—at least my eyes and mouth. She said she'd do it. She'd fix it all for me tomorrow.

Are you sure? I said. It can be sort of tricky if you haven't done it before.

I'm not worried, she said. Then maybe we can get a candle going in there again.

Maybe. It's not super comfortable though.

But it looks so cool.

Then she was shoving me out the back door, allowing me only a single flat kiss, her lips set firmly against her teeth. I took her by her elastic waistband and pulled her tightly to me, then ran my hand into her pink work scrubs. She grabbed my wrist and gave it a sharp squeeze.

Maybe tomorrow, she said. I can't be distracted right now.

Shit, I said. Tomorrow is forever.

Not really, she said. So I guess I'll borrow my friend's loppers. Is that a good way to do it?

Sure, I said, for the stalk.

I left her house. My wife would want to know what made me so late. Yesterday I told her a gravel hauler tipped over on the highway. I was stuck. Of course, my wife is smart, a lot smarter than me. So there's only so much shit I can get away with. When I finally got home, my little pumpkin-head boys were on the porch cheering for me. Daddy's home! Then they started punching each other before I even climbed the steps. By the time I got my first beer open, they were crying, and my wife was pissed at them and at me, as usual. The highway was a disaster, I said. I did my best to look exhausted.

After dinner, I didn't yell at the kids or say mean things to my wife. I cleaned up the table and scrubbed out the burned scum from the pots and put the boys to bed. Then finally, I fell asleep on the couch in front of the TV.

The next day was forever long. I climbed ladders and painted windows all afternoon. The leaves were gone from the trees and it was quieter now when the wind blew, but then it blew harder and the trees whistled with it and the hollow rungs of my aluminum ladder hummed.

At four, I told my boss that my wife had called to say that my youngest was sick and that I needed to pick up some medicine.

OK, he said. You better get to it.

I really don't have a choice, I said. So I cleaned my brush, jumped in my car, and drove straight to Cindy's place. I dashed up her steps and pounded on her door. She was just back from work too and still wearing her pink scrubs. She asked me in but instead of hugging me she backed up and sat in front of her computer screen and began typing.

Got to finish this email to my boss, she said.

I sat at her table and waited, tapping my fingers.

So, she said finally. What's up?

I reminded her about my stalk.

Oh, that's right. Damn it. I forgot to get the loppers from my friend. She looked around and found a big flimsy kitchen knife. I can do it with this, she said.

That'll probably work.

She wrapped a towel over my shoulders and put one in my lap. The knife was a dull, cheap thing with a rusted edge. I felt its point dig into my head.

That sort of hurts, I said.

Really, I didn't think you could feel that.

Yeah, I feel it. It works a lot better with a sharp knife. This just feels very weird.

She leaned hard on the handle and forced the cold metal all the way into my skull.

There, she said, and she sawed and sawed until she got all the way around. She took my stalk and wiggled it just slightly and the small lid that she had made popped open with a satisfying sucking sound. She set it aside and gave me a damp cloth to wipe my face.

The weird thing about it was I was glad she was touching me, even if it hurt. Her hands were small and strong and amazing. She brought out a big slotted spoon and dug around inside my head and scraped out all the seedy gunk and stringy pulp that had grown there, then dropped it into a big plastic bucket.

What am I supposed to do with this stuff?

Throw it in the trash. It's no big deal, I said.

She stood in front of me and held my face steady while she examined her work. When she was done, she took the candle from her nightstand—the rose-scented one that she had been burning that day we both called in sick and sprawled in her bed, exhausted from our all-afternoon fuck fest. She lit the wick and plunked the candle into the new dry cavity of my head. The flame warmed me, but got hot quick. A stream of waxy smoke drifted from my eye cuts. She stood back and looked at me.

That's pretty good, she said. But, hmm, I'd better fix the left eye.

She stuck the knife in there and cleaned up a rough edge. That's much better, she said.

I stood. I felt dizzy. I was a new man with a new mouth and new nose and new eyes. I was Cindy's man. I brushed the stringy pulp from my legs. She took the towels outside and shook them from her porch, and orange blobs shot off into the neighbor's yard.

I looked in the mirror. Oh, Jesus, I said. She had gouged me good. I felt suddenly hollow and terrible. She had changed my eyes and nose to triangles. She had given me a jagged toothy mouth. I knew this was going to be trouble with my wife. Still, I almost didn't care. I just needed to kiss Cindy in the worst sort of way. I pursed my lips, but because of the asymmetrical cut she had made, I was having a hard time putting them together. I reached for her waist. I needed to pull off her pinks. I needed to slip past the elastic and the little fabric tie that held her clothes together. I needed to yank everything off her and love every part of her smooth hilly body with every part of mine. For a second, she let me rest my hand on her breast. Then she shoved it away.

We can't do that anymore, she said.

I pushed my mouth against her cheek and tried to kiss her.

I can't kiss you either, she said. I'm sorry, but there's a hundred reasons why I can't.

That's not fair, I said. It was weird hearing my voice. It sounded strangely dry and slurred. The new cut of my mouth made everything come out wrong.

She laughed at me and shook her head. I wanted to slap her and kiss her, then slap her again, but she turned away. She was looking over my shoulder at her computer.

Sorry, she said. I just can't.

Her control was sudden and astonishing. How could she just stop? I didn't know what to do. I should be kissing her. That's what we do together. That's what we've done since the day I stayed late, painting her place, and she invited me in for a beer. Finally I said, Do you really think I look OK?

Better, she said. Authentic, at least.

You won't kiss me, really? I pleaded.

Jeez, she said. Do I have to spell it out for you. I can't anymore. It's not fair to me. Now I really don't want to talk about it.

God damn, I said, God damn, God damn. Fuck. I wish you could have told me before I let you cut me all up. I would have just gone to my barber. Now look at me. You cored me. What am I going to tell my wife? You gave me fucking triangle eyes!

You look better, she said.

Yeah, right! I stormed out of her house and off her porch. I got in my car and I drove and drove, feeling terrible, not thinking, ripping around the neighborhood. Then I turned onto I-75 and was immediately stuck in traffic. At first I thought it was due to some accident, but then I realized it was something very different.

Cars had pulled over and all sorts of people were just wandering between the vehicles, walking the white lines, and then bending over and scooping stuff up, even combing through the grass and half-dead landscaping of the embankment. It was a very weird scene. No one was going anywhere, and then I realized why. A hundred dollar bill hit my windshield, then blew past me. My God, a hundred! I rolled down my window and glanced out. There it was, just wedged under my back tire. I opened my door and un-crinked my body and reached for the bill, but then a man in greasy blue coveralls grabbed it. We glanced at each other.

Holy Jesus, he said, and he walked quickly away.

What a fucked-up day, I said. I got back in my car and watched the people weaving feverishly between vehicles, scanning the pavement. Traffic wasn't going to be moving anytime soon, so I edged my car onto the shoulder of the highway.

As I opened my door, the wind cut through the holes in my face. It felt cool and foreign on the inner walls of my head. It sharpened the day and swiftly blew the flame off Cindy's candle. I walked up the hill. All those people, some still in their cars, all were looking at me but pretending not to. A helicopter was hovering above the scene, cutting up the air, filming us for one TV station or another. I could feel its camera on me. I was embarrassed and disappointed in myself and in Cindy too.

Then just before I reached the bridge, I saw a hundred stuck in a scrubby bush. I folded it up and put it in my pocket. I thought of Cindy first. I wanted to go straight to her house. I wanted to tell her the good news about the money. I wanted to spend it all as quickly as possible. I called her.

I can't talk now, she said.

I told her about the hundred.

Look, I'm in a dinner meeting with my boss.

What dinner meeting? I said.

Yeah, I can't talk now. Call me tomorrow or something.

That's when I realized what was up. Of course she didn't want to see me later or probably ever again. She didn't even care about what a dumb carving job she did on me. She was probably just glad to have me out of her house.

I walked past a closed factory at the edge of the city. Just months ago it was a mess of activity—trucks blocked the road, little carts zipped people from one end of the complex to the other. Now the place was empty except for a security guard sleeping in his pickup. I ended up stopping at Kelly's Bar. The place used to be full of factory workers. Now there was a For Sale sign in the high window over the entrance.

At the far end of the bar, the only patron, an old man with almost no teeth, glanced at me, then turned his attention back to the TV. They were having a Breaking News Alert. Apparently an armored truck had lost a big sack of money on the highway. Its rear door had busted open and the money bag flipped out and one car hit it and then another and bills flew and swirled. The newsman described it: In a desperate neighborhood pounded by recession and factory closings, this scene is one of gleeful chaos. He went on to say that the armored truck company had released a statement saying that anyone who returned the cash wouldn't be prosecuted. They showed an aerial shot of the scene, and zeroed in on one man grabbing and stuffing money in his pocket.

Lucky fucking day, the old man said.

The bartender shook his head. We could sure use some of that cash right now.

I spread my hundred on the counter.

The bartender looked at me. How about that? He laughed. What are you drinking, my friend?

A shot of Jezy and a beer, I said. Make it a round of shots for all of us.

Alright, he said, and he grabbed me a High Life and popped the top and set three glasses on the bar and poured three very friendly shots.

I swore off this stuff months ago, he said. Can't seem to quit drinking it though. He smiled.

We raised our glasses together and clinked. *Skal, na zdrowie,* cheers! Their eyes looked as red as mine felt.

Let's do that again, I said.

The bartender nodded. He poured three more shots.

I took the lid from my head and pulled out Cindy's candle and re-lit it with some bar matches. I burned my hand replacing it. The pain was sharp and direct, but far fucking better than heartache. I tried to smile but the face Cindy gave me was so damn stiff. I probably should have got up right then and gone to see my barber. Maybe he could fix her mess, erase the dumb mark she had left on me. It was like I was wearing her fuck flag. Like my wife wouldn't know something was up? When I got home she was going to say, What the hell happened to you? For years we had spent all this time trying to blend in, trying to look like we belonged here. Now I looked just like a fucking jack-o'-lantern.

In the mirror behind the bar, I barely recognized myself. My head glowed brightly with a strong yellow flame. A rose-scented smoke lifted from my eyeholes and the heat blurred my vision. What am I doing? I said.

You want another? the bartender said.

No, I said. I've got to roll.

I killed my beer and left a twenty on the bar.

Thanks, the bartender yelled after me.

Just outside the wind whipped into my eyes. It took the flame right off Cindy's candle. Almost instantly, my head cooled. I grabbed my stalk, lifted my lid, and plucked out the stupid thing. Melted wax ran down my wrist with a sharp heat. I stepped back and hurled that pink, rose-scented lump of shit as far as I could. It landed across the street, next to a dumpster, and split in two like a small, soft skull. I took a deep breath. Even the exhaust of the passing trucks was better than the perfumed stink of that candle.

Only Wilma

I didn't know there were cowboys in Detroit, she says.

Not too many, I tell her.

Real Cowboys? she says. What are you, like a circus cowboy?

No.

Rodeo?

Here I am, a novelty to all, depressed, anxious, sitting at the long wooden bar. Since taking my stool, I've devoted my attention to Big Wilma, who sways in her skirt, delivering shots and beers. Maybe I'm wrong, but with arms as thick as hers, it seems she'd have no trouble launching anyone who gets out of hand—belligerent or drunk, with the face of a sledgehammer—and simply catapult them into the night. Plus, she's a solid beauty. From the moment I laid eyes on this woman, I wanted to kiss her.

I point to my glass, my hand shaking, not from nerves but from my prescription pills. They mess with me, but I need them, or I might just stay up all night. I've done that before for seven nights in a row. The eighth, I've always heard, will kill you. That's usually the day I end up in the hospital.

Another one of those for you, cowboy? Wilma asks.

I tip my hat and thank her for her hospitality. I know I am drinking more than I should and ought to get riding out of here. My borrowed, sort of stolen piebald horse, dearest Squint Eye, is probably tired of being tethered to the ice cooler, probably anxious about the headlights, and the blacktop that's in such disrepair and not so good for hooves. Sure, it's fine for parking cars, but horses do better with a trough, some hay or something.

An hour later, I am still drinking. It appears that I have outlasted all the other patrons. She leans over the bar, looking at the guns that ride at my side.

Whatcha got there? she says.

I pull my Colt single-action army revolvers from their holsters, relieving myself of their weight, and let them sit on the bar between us.

Wow those look old, she says. Do they work?

I nod. Yep. They were my grandfather's. Check them out. The leather holsters and belt are stamped and patterned with swirly Wild West designs, which I've decided might be representations of cloud formations or air movement. I have oiled them to no end, but the rot continues eating away at the leather. Soon they may tear in two, but until then they are very cool. Maybe the coolest things I own.

Apparently, Big Wilma is about to close up the place. She tells me it's time for cowboys to take their shooters and ride off into the sunset or moonrise or whatever's out there.

At this latitude in northern Michigan, the sun is up late and turns the sky an eerie pink for a long time before it sinks below the horizon, but of course by now it has long set. It's dark as hell out there. I can't stand the thought of leaving her. Really, I don't have anywhere good to go. Sooner or later I'm going to get caught sneaking into the hayloft at the Lakeside Equestrian Resort. Not allowed. It makes me nervous, but nothing feels quite as bad as leaving her.

Hey Wilma, um, all night I've been thinking how it might be to kiss you.

Hmm. Really?

Yep.

I don't know, Bill. You seem pretty nice, and this cowboy thing you have going is kind of cute, but I really don't get it.

It's who I am.

Obviously. Well OK, gimme a kiss. Then get your ass out of here.

I lean across the bar and plant one on her sweet red lips. It's slow and tender and lasts surprisingly long.

Hmm. She nods in appreciation. You know, she says, I guess I could use some company. I just gotta get out of this dump. Give me a hand with the cleanup, and we'll have a couple drinks at my place.

SHE HAPPENS TO reside upstairs from the bar. I remove my hat and follow her down a dimly lit hall. She produces a key. Well, she says, be prepared for a bit of a mess.

All right, no problem.

I'm surprised to see that Big Wilma's apartment is so small, only an efficiency, barely any space for her dresser, a table, and a bed. There's clutter everywhere.

Upon our entry, a fly crawls zigzag on the windowpane and then launches itself, circling the light in a lazy flight, and bumps into my forehead. I snag it from the air and toss it against the floor, where it sputters on its back. Oh Jeez. I'm sorry about that. It's a living thing. Certainly, I have injured it. I didn't mean to. It was just a knee-jerk reaction. I scoop the little guy up and set it on the windowsill.

Goddamn flies, she says. They drive me crazy. This place sucks. I'm trying to buy my Daddy's farm and get out of here, but so far it's not working. You want to kiss me again?

I do.

We press our lips together in the same nice way we did across the bar. Only now our bodies are touching. I can feel the wondrous curve of her belly as it weighs heavily against my belt buckle. She squeezes me and pulls me against the fleshy heave of her breasts. If it were not for the softness of every part of her, she might just break me right in two.

Then Wilma steps back and unzips her skirt, with a loud zzzzz-rup! She tosses it across the room to a chair that apparently doubles as her hamper.

Should I get out of my clothes too? I say.

Yeah. It's time to let your skin breathe.

OK, then. I undo my holsters, set my Colts near the door, open my dungarees and let them fall, unbutton my embroidered shirt and lay it over the arm of her chair, already draped with a layer of skirts, shirts, huge bras. Suddenly I'm aware of my past-due need for a bath. Of course there is no laundry or shower at the Lakeside Equestrian Resort, only a hose and soap bucket that can be dragged into each stable.

I sigh with appreciation as Wilma removes her top, exposing her big bazoombas and beer keg of a belly. Her skin is tanned, tea-colored, with the white imprint of a bikini.

Dang! I say. She dips. She swells, so heavy and round, so big in every bone, so muscular.

Dang, what?

You're amazing.

She looks at me in my tighty-whities, which currently have some sag to them. She doesn't return the compliment. Instead she asks if I'm really from Detroit proper or just some sort of suburb? And what the hell am I doing up here anyway?

I'm from Novi, I say. It's not real close to the city, but I'm pretty sure it qualifies as the Metro Detroit area. I think.

What's in Novi?

Nothing. They don't call it Some-vi. They call it No-vi.

Ha! So what are you doing up here?

I like it up here.

Hmm. I guess it's alright. I really want to see Detroit someday. I heard it's cool. I have an old friend who lives there.

It's a mess still. I don't know about Detroit.

She removes her remaining undergarments and runs water in the corner sink, then wets a hand towel and washes her face and neck and stomach and posterior.

OK. Your turn, she says. Give yourself a scrub, cowboy.

Alright. Thank you.

She hands me a washrag, then climbs into bed. It feels awfully good to clean up. I soap up and towel dry. I'm almost not nervous anymore but the jitters are still there just below the surface. Finally, I join her in the sack, where together we enjoy a drink of Canadian Club. It's very nice here. I rest my head on her pillows, which carry a pleasant feminine odor, a scent of soap and perfumed powders and lavender mists.

We take turns holding the bottle to our lips. The whiskey warms my gullet and somehow makes me feel like a better cowboy. With the taste still in my mouth, she kisses me, climbs on top, blocks out the light, and we ease into the sweetest moments I have ever known.

I might be really fucking confused about my life, but I'm certainly happy about being here in this little room, lying in bed with this round, wonderful gal. I try for sleep. It should come but won't. It doesn't take long before she is snoozing with light snores and occasional grunts. I remain awake for hours, my brain going a hundred thousand miles an hour. I keep tugging on the bottle, hoping for some calm. Can't get the damn brain to stop. I lie still. I stay put, waiting for some sort of respite.

It's still dark and I only have just dozed when she wakes and wants to do it all again. Of course I'm game. I'm in love. I'm a little drunk too. I'm dead serious as I hold her breasts and ask if she might consider joining me in wedlock.

Marry you? She flicks on the light, smiles just a little, gets out of bed nude and massive, and then shuts the bathroom door and urinates loudly. Well, I'll do it, she says from behind the door. But you're gonna have to buy my father's farm. Then I will. I'll marry you. We can live there. I'm serious. Are you?

THE FOLLOWING MORNING, I'm hungover, but not unhappy. I take up my shovel and ride Squint Eye, my trusty piebald, beautifully mottled brown and white coarse hair, strong and sweating beneath me. We head into the woods and through the meadow, where the creek flows to the Wolf river, where the grass is tall and seed-heavy, and fern and moss cling to the shade of the birch and pine. Everything shines with dew.

The water is full of fish racing upstream. Their bodies are all muscle and smooth, shining silver scale. They rise against the current and throw themselves forward over slimy, rust-streaked stones.

Ten feet from the water's edge, and five feet from the dead pine with wrist-thick ropes of poison ivy strangling its trunk, I jab my hand shovel into the dirt and work, until a foot below grade, I hit the metal box that I stashed just over a week ago. I brush away the dirt and extract a Ziploc bag holding enough cash for what will only amount to a meager payment on Wilma's family farm. I don't care that I know nothing about what to do with earth or seed or livestock of any kind, nor am I versed in repairing leaky roofs or busted plaster. I count the bills, but as many times as I try, I keep coming up with different numbers. It should be five thousand. The hundreds feel weird in my hand.

IS IT NOT a testimony of my love, true love, that I don't need to see the farm to know I need to buy it? Well, it turns out her father is truly wasted, wheelchair-ridden, side-saddle oxygen tanks and tubes plugged into his nose. She rolls the decrepit man onto the veranda of the nursing home. Despite his condition, he shows some real eagerness regarding my cash. Together we three sit at a plastic table and fill in the blanks of the land contract. Upon signing, Big Wilma kisses me, almost knocking me off my chair. Suddenly I have a house and a wife of sorts. On our way out of there, she says we need to christen every room and outbuilding with ceremonial sex. I agree completely.

We head to the farm, me on horseback, she in her pickup truck. I lead Squint Eye through the high grass on the side of the road and into a stretch of government-owned land, where I drop low against her withers, ducking the branches that smack past us. My thighs burn with the work of balancing and setting squeeze to her belly. Despite Squint Eye's damaged ocular sense, she can still travel with speed and grace. I love her, I say. I love everything. We pick up the pace and finally arrive.

All I can say is I'm surprised. The place is a disaster. I try not to let it bother me. Maybe it doesn't matter that the barn is sloped, hunched, a little broken-backed. Its vertical siding is hanging from rusty nailheads and swinging in the wind. I lead Squint Eye through the spiderwebs, over the rat droppings, and into a stall, and pitch a forkful of alfalfa at her feet. She is blinking at me. She seems stunned. Her eyes are watering too.

Yes, I guess I'm crazy, I say. Yes, I'm crazy.

I stroke her neck and talk with as much calm and reassurance as I can muster, apologizing about the new accommodations. Her ears swivel on her head. I know that this is no Lakeside Equestrian Resort, for sure.

Unfortunately, the land is not much better than the structures sitting on it. The soy crop is bedraggled and rife with weeds and bug-eaten.

Amen to Wilma! She keeps her word about christening the place. She stands in the doorway of the house, completely nude. Her hair, no longer knotted in a bun, now flows down her neck, over the torrential slope of breasts. That afternoon, we accomplish more than I have in most of my young adult life. We do it in both bedrooms, in the kitchen, and by the time we hit the living room, I'm exhausted but manage to keep up with her somehow. Yes, we hit every room, managing all sorts of positions and sexual achievements. Makes me wonder if this has ever been done before. I think we are touching on some world record. We end the day in the shower together, washing the slime of lube from our skin. You know, she says, passing me the soap, I don't see any reason to go through the ceremony of marrying. I mean it's just a piece of paper.

I'm happy this way, I say. Everything is good.

We continue celebrating our love and friendship with daily sex and whiskey. For at least a month, everything about life seems absolutely perfect.

THEN EVERYTHING CHANGES. It starts when a man raps on the glass of the front door with a loud impertinent knock. I don't know who the hell he is or why he might be here, wearing a suit and tie, with an expensive looking haircut. Even his clean-shaven cheeks make me sick with worry. Before I can rise from my chair, he opens the door and booms his big voice into the house, calling for Wilma. Though I have never shot anything—except my own leg, a grazing wound—my instinct is to pull my Colt revolvers.

I'm totally caught off guard when Wilma squeals his name. Oh Leo! She welcomes him with a disgusting kiss on the lips.

Don't worry, she says to me. I've known Leo since I was five.

She invites him into the kitchen and sits him at our table, asking if he wants her to make some coffee.

Look at this, he says, opening his briefcase and extracting two expensive looking bottles of whiskey, a brand I've never seen. If you both are up for it, he says, I'd like to have a drink. Let's have some drinks. OK?

Though it's only three in the afternoon, it does sound good. Wilma has the day off, so we crack open the bottles, and I do my best to reserve my skepticism about this man and begin drinking.

Leo is rich, she says.

Hmm, I say, and nod.

I can't deny it, he says. I got rich in Detroit. Crazy-ass city. You'd never think there's money to be made there, but there is.

That's weird, I say. I look over at Wilma. She seems a little skeptical too.

As we drink, he gets talking about his job. It's through this bank. He's doing something he calls "reacquisitions." The more I listen, the more it sounds like he's booting people from their houses.

Yeah, he says, it's all about contracts. Some people don't understand contracts. You can read them right out loud in front of their face and they still don't get it. They'll sign anything. Then they don't hold up their end, and suddenly I gotta deal with them. I gotta ask for the house back. Sometimes it's hard enforcing a contract. I feel their pain, but also somebody has to do it, and frankly I get a pretty good cut. It's crazy. Now there's so much work for our department that I can just barely keep up. I got a whole staff working for me. It's something. Really something down there in Detroit! You know Wilma, I could really use your brain for numbers. I'm serious. You could make a ton of dough. You should come down and work for me. I could use a gal like you. You too Bill.

I don't know about that, I say. So you know Wilma from way back?

Well, yes, I do. She and I have a brief glorious history all right. He pauses and looks back and forth across the table at our hands. Are you married or something? I don't see any rings.

Well, sort of.

Sort of! Here's to sort of! He raises his glass.

All I know is things are out of control here. Maybe she's just drunk, but my Big Wilma actually seems interested in Leo's offer. Soon she is up and heating the cast iron pan and draping strips of bacon over it. The first thing she has cooked in weeks.

Even drunk on his fancy whiskey, I can't stand to look at this Leo character. Finally, I slam down my glass, get up, and walk out of the house.

I spend the rest of the day doing target practice, shooting at paper bull's-eyes that I stapled to a tree. I keep waiting to be a deadeye marksman. So far it's not happening. I can't tell if the whiskey steadies my hand or makes it worse.

IN THE DAYS following Leo's visit, Wilma speaks of him with a wistful glaze in her eyes. She tells me that she is really curious about this job he was talking about. It might be a way to make some cash to pay daddy everything, then owe nothing on this place, no land contract. Nothing.

I'm confused by everything. Drunk again, and maybe I took too many pills today, or got the order wrong. I don't know. There's the ones that make me stay awake. The ones that make me sleep. The ones that are supposed to level me so my heart doesn't jump out of my fucking chest and run screaming down the road. The ones for my stomach, and the last one just to round out the rest. I can't remember what it does, but it's small and triangular and blue.

I wake early the next morning, very groggy, still in the heavy mud of sleep, and I'm pretty sure she has just kissed me and is telling me she's going, really going, but I don't get it. I can't wake to tell her so. In my dream she is wearing a smart skirt and a blouse with the open collar fitting snugly around her breasts. Even in my semi-conscious state, she is undeniably lovely. Next I know, the floorboards are creaking, and she is leaving the room. The door of our land-contract house is closing loudly, the key is twisting in the lock, the bolt thumping into place. Next, the engine of her pickup truck is turning over. I'm trying to believe it's not true. There's no way she is leaving. Aren't I her husband? I drift back into sleep only to wake hours later in the dead quiet of the empty house. Unable to rise.

I don't know if I ever really understood the word "heartbreak," only that now I am suffering. It's two completely black days before I realize the sullen gravity of my situation. With her gone, I am ragged and blank and only faintly able to recognize myself in the mirror. I rise in the cool afternoon air but only to put the cold barrel of one of grandpa's Colt revolvers to my head. The pain of loss is so great. It sucks at my heart, pulling away all my blood. I walk myself into a badly dwarfed soy crop that I did not plant or tend to, that was probably only seeded by shitting birds, pure chance that it grows at all. I lie shivering in the leaves, looking at the sky and its dust of dim light, speckling, haze. I am unbathed but for the rain on my face. If it were not for Squint Eye and the care I know she needs, I might give up altogether.

After three miserable days, I enter the house one last time, in the full blur of hangover, seeing only dust, cobwebs, food-stuck plates, and two empty bottles of unaffordable whiskey. I gather my pack and prescription pill bottles. I turn and walk from the empty building into my broken-down barn. I saddle Squint Eye, my sweet piebald, stroke her neck and tell her it's time. We're going to be OK. We're going to be alright.

A storm is brewing to the north, but the sky to the south is still clear. My direction is obvious. We ride the rolling hills to the south end of my property, over the creek that leads to the Wolf river, and off to the county road, leading south. Behind me, a tower of ominous clouds rises over my land, spiraling upward, until finally at a great height it spreads out across the heavens. Not a mile away, and I can't remember if I have closed the door properly. I worry another mile over it, then I turn back to check the lock. I take it as a good sign that I have remembered to flip the bolt, then begin my journey again.

IN TWO DAYS' time, I make acceptable progress, but end up at a roadside bar not far from the rocky shores of Lake Huron. I stay through the afternoon trying to drink away the terrible ache that has built in my chest. Somehow, I'm low on cash. The bartender is uncertain about me using my mom's debit card, but ultimately allows it and lets me get some cash back too.

I may be delirious, but at least I know how to pick a good bar. I'm about to leave when the bartender introduces me to Esteban, moonshine maker, traveler, assistant to those in need. He has climbed out of some underground storage area, and seems to understand my plight before I explain a thing. The bar is dark and getting darker. Soon there will be no light at all. He says he can help us, me and my horse, gain safe passage to Detroit. I put my glass down, noting something deeply spiritual about this place, this man, his black robe, weathered red cheeks, long uncombed hair, rangy beard, and blue penetrating eyes. The kindness he extends makes me cry. I agree to his terms.

Soon, I am looking out over the water and the gray waves of Lake Huron. My horse chews what little grass surrounds us. Her saddlebags carry no treats, only a family pack of baloney, canned beans, tortilla shells, a dog-eared map of Michigan, a handful of bullets, and of course all my pill bottles.

Finally Esteban and the motorized barge arrives, but not until the night has achieved a sullen pitch. He greets me with a pat on the back and explains the terms again. I pay him the two hundred in twenties. He guides my horse up the steep metal planking against the breeze, the waves now capped with foam. The motor, an Evinrude Outboard, 60hp, loud as hell, emits a blue exhaust, and we push into the murky waters, heading toward the power plants of Sarnia. I blanket Squint Eye, covering her head, and I stroke her velvet muzzle. Her legs are alive with jitters. It will take more than a day, but at least I won't have to navigate the highways. It's better this way, I tell her. She has no response, but she seems to understand.

BY NIGHTFALL OF the following day, we approach the Motor City, with its handful of tall buildings clustered together and hovering over the river, concrete and glass; in all of them people are doing work that makes no sense. Leo maybe is in one of them, conniving to take over block after block of the city. And who knows, maybe Wilma is with him too. God help me if her legs, so large and lovely, are spread in sick appreciation of this man and his stunning wealth. I am ripped in half by this image. I force it away. It's not fair. I cannot allow myself to think this way.

Over the course of the trip, Esteban has become a good friend and advisor. I confide in him about Wilma. His face is worn with understanding. He nods and tells me to forget her. She is a worthless slut. It's painful even hearing those words. This is my wife, I say. This is the love of my life. I can't let her go.

Ah, I see. He nods gravely. I think he does see. His eyes hold a worried foreboding of some terrible looming future. Then he lifts his head and smiles. You will find her, he says. I am certain. She will be your wife again.

The barge comes to a jerking halt, pushed up on a short stretch of sand, amid huge boulders. This is it, my friend, he says. I can go no further.

He gives me a strong hug, slapping my shoulders repeatedly, then pats Squint Eye on the ass and throws down the gangway. Off you go. *Vaya con Dios.* And watch for the Border Patrol. They are all impenetrable idiots, eager to prove their worth. Move quickly away from shore and do your best to remain undetected. *Vaya con Dios,* my friend.

I MOUNT SQUINT Eye and we clomp away from the river. She seems so pleased to be on dry land. I don't blame her. The barge ride was long, very tedious for a horse to endure. Here we are in Detroit on a broken sidewalk surrounded by weeds.

We head into what looks like it was once a neighborhood. A streetlight flickers on and then off again. Though we are here, we are lost already. Aware only that we are moving away from the river. It's dark. So dark. So late. And I have no plan, no direction, only I know we need to stop and rest. I let Squint Eye lead. She steers us off the pavement and takes us through a field. We end up near the banks of a small pond where she wades and waters herself. In the light from the little slice of moon, I can see shimmery ripples radiating from my horse's legs. They extend to a small garage and into the yards of three delinquent houses. One of them is burned, and fingers of its charred timbers rise into the air, roof completely gone. It must hurt to be this house. This is a terrible sad place, but I am exhausted and cannot go another step, nor can I force Squint Eye to move. She is tired and has locked her legs. I decide this is as good a place as any to set up camp for the night.

I am so lonely. I miss Wilma. I really miss her. Without her I am so cruddy and hollow and desperate to sleep in our old bed and press my head against her shoulder and let her stroke my hair.

BEFORE I KNOW it, the morning has arrived. I wake to the sound of many chirping insects. I'm watching the birds zing overhead. They watch me too, their heads twitching with loud chirps. They perch everywhere except the burned house. They watch me as I make a fire pit, stripping a circle of vegetation and digging into the black soil.

After breakfast of tortilla shells and hot chili beans, we abandon camp and move on, heading northeast. My only lead on Wilma this whole time has been a slip of paper with Leo's number and extension, carrying the logo of the bank where he works. I've consulted my map and located the street, Jos. Campau. I lead Squint Eye in this direction and begin the final leg of our trip, now clomping off the pavement into the alleyways, which are unused, overgrown, better for horses. The closer we get to our destination, the more I'm required to ride the streets and deal with traffic. There's not much, but those that drive have no sense of traffic law. Squint Eye remains steady, but I understand what it means when she whinnies and her skin twitches. She is not happy about being here. We skirt a factory. Trains bang together. Broken glass covers the sidewalk. She whinnies again.

At last, we arrive in a somewhat densely populated area of the city. Rows of shops line the street, many of them empty, some carrying signs in the windows for Clearance Sales. Cars continue honking and drive quickly past, issuing curses. We come to a halt across the street from what appears to be a fortress made of sandstone, wind-worn like a desert plateau, its edges melted away perhaps by the polluted rain of the city, which streaked its walls for years. The ride has been trying. I dismount and tether Squint Eye to a pole, then decide against it and walk her around to the alley. I won't be long, I say. Wish me luck. As I cross the street, a gusty wind sends bits of trash swirling past my feet.

Finally, I enter the glass doors of the bank with pounding heart and move forward through the vestibule with its sign about removing hoods and hats and sunglasses, and I push through the next set of doors and I am standing in the lobby trying to get my bearings. Above me, the giant domed ceiling is decorated with green and golden frieze work. Truly impressive.

An old man dressed in a suit with hair oiled and dragged over his balding crown is pitched forward at the information desk. He narrows his eyes on my guns and signals the security guard who is moving toward me with fast steps. A bulky black pistol rides on his belt.

Sir, he says, with his hand on his holster, flicking open his strap. He is removing his weapon and holding it at his side. Excuse me sir, he says. You can't come in here with heat like that, even if they're not real. Everyone will think you're trying to rob the place.

Oh, I say. I'm only here to find my wife. Her name is Wilma, goes by Big Wilma.

Sir, are you listening? Sir, you're going to need to go back to your car. You cannot do business in this building with those weapons on your belt.

What about Leo? Is he here?

At the mention of this name the guard nods and relaxes his stance a little. Sir, he says. Remove your gear or I'm launching you out of here.

I know my hands are trembling, which is not a good sign. I'm doing my best to unhitch my belt when Leo, with his coiffed hair, lotioned face, and shining grin, comes gliding out of his office. He crosses through the lobby with a handful of papers and a coffee, and I can feel all the hairs on my back stand on end and prick alive.

Oh, hello Cowboy Bill, he says in his boomy voice. How goes the rodeo—Just kidding pal. Good to see you. He nods to the guard. I've got it, Terry. This is Bill. He's one of the good guys, right Bill? Yeah, just do leave your pistols with Terry here. He'll take good care of them. Let's go have a sit-down.

I'm looking for Wilma.

Oh what a gal! I love her. Wow! C'mon. Let's sit down.

On our way to his office, we pass the counter with its row of tellers doling out cash. No sign of Wilma among them.

Come on, Billy Boy. Wow, you're all sweaty.

I rode my horse here. It wasn't easy.

All the way to Detroit. Wow. I'm impressed.

He guides me to his office, past his secretary, who is thin as a fashion model, but pretty as she is, she has nothing on Wilma. How can a woman like this keep anything warm? Just thinking it, a sharp pain twists beneath my ribs.

Leo tells his secretary to come in just for a moment.

Well, Bill, he says, I guess you've had some time to consider my offer. Good to see you. Wow, what a week of visitors we've had! First your Wilma and now you. We're just having a time of it, aren't we, Miss Griffin?

Sure Leo, she says, your friends are really something.

Hey Miss Griffin, why don't you bring us some of that summer sausage? There's some of that around still, isn't there? And see if there isn't some cheese too.

Sure, she says. She closes the door behind her.

So Bill, he says, You're going to like this sausage. Terry, our security guard, made it. It's got jalapenos in it. Good stuff.

I don't care for sausage, I say. Where can I find Wilma? Is she here? My voice has got away from me and is pitched with a high strain. I know I'm not yelling but I'm close. Where is she?

Whoa horsey, keep it down, he says. Spinning his chair, he retrieves one of his fancy bottles of executive-grade whiskey, pops the cork, and begins pouring.

I need to know.

Jeez. Sit down. Come on. You're making me nervous. Let's have a drink together in the spirit of brotherhood. He opens a small refrigerator and fills each of the tumblers with ice. You like it iced? I do. I like it cold. Cold is good. Let's drink to Wilma. So big, but what a woman. My God!

I'm just asking for some very simple information. I'm not here to drink.

You gotta have a drink.

I'm not thinking anymore. My body has coiled so tight and my muscles ache to move. I am not an athletic person or a gymnast, but I am full up to my eyes with his bullshit and can no longer stand the sight of him. Suddenly, I'm on my feet. I'm leaning over his desk.

Could you please just tell me where she is?

What the fuck, Bill? Chill out.

I can't take it any longer. I snap. I totally lose my shit. I spring right over his desk, going for his neck. My fingers come together on his smooth skin, which feels small and boneless in my grip. I'm circling his throat and pushing his pipes together until his face is red and his little eyes are swelling from their sockets.

Tell me. Where is she? Tell me.

He chokes and wheezes.

I let up for just a second.

Fuck you, Bill! What kind of shit is this? I only offered you a job. He buckles over and begins coughing.

Where is she? I say it again. Tell me!

He pushes me away, holding his arm out to stop me, but I'm ready to strangle him again.

I step toward him, and he flinches, backing up fast, and flips his chair over, which snags the printer cord and yanks the telephone line too, and down they go with a loud crash.

You idiot, he says. She went back north already.

What?!

That's right you idiot. If you just had a fucking cell phone like the rest of us, you could have called her and asked. Instead you ride around on your stupid horse like it's the 1800s. You didn't need to strangle me. He coughs and spits a wad of something on the carpet. It didn't work out. I don't know how you live with that woman. She may have the best ass from here to California, but she's crazy as a loon. You two blockheads are made for each other.

Me? Us?

Yes, you! You idiot.

I can feel tears welling in me. My vision is blurred and I wipe my eyes with the back of my hand. My breathing has turned to blubbering. I need only to see her so badly.

Just then, Miss Griffin comes walking in with the sausage tray and sees us both red and sweating. Why is the printer on the floor? Are you OK?

Bill here just blew a cog. Please get Terry.

I glance at the summer sausage she left on his desk. Its pungent odor fills the room. It sits proud next to a wedge of cheese and a bowl of dates.

I look at Leo and his slobbering eyes and know I need to get out of here.

Without knowing why, I grab the sausage and run from the room. Thankfully Terry is nowhere to be seen. Only the old man from the information desk is coming toward me, but I whip past him. I'm looking around for my gun belt as I run through the main room, like it might be hanging on the cowboy gun check rack or something, but there's no time to find it, and I know I might just be in a huge amount of trouble here, and my blood is racing, pounding in my ears, so I keep going.

There is no one blocking my exit but a group of stunned women. I ask them to please excuse me, and push past, and make it through the glass doors. The sun is shining still, alive with light and hovering high over the buildings in the clear blue sky. I sprint down the sidewalk, holding my hat on my head, moving faster than I have in years.

I round the back of the post office and into the alley where Squint Eye is hitched to a chain-link fence. She is shifting from hoof to hoof. I know she's upset. Everything is going to be OK, I say. Just give me a minute. She snorts and I spin the dial on the combination lock and pop the U-bolt and pull the cable and coil it into the saddlebags and then mount her. All it takes is one sharp kick to the belly, and she jolts with energy in a quick, graceful gallop.

I continue looking over my shoulder but there is no pursuer. No police siren. Nothing. After a good mile, I rein her in. Somehow, maybe, they're letting us get away.

I know we have a long way to go. Suddenly here we are at the entrance to the interstate, which runs in a deep cement trench, heading directly north, right where we need to go. I contemplate the ramp, but know it's a risky choice, all those cars and semi-trucks and us with no taillights. I veer away. Stick to my instincts.

I'm riding fast through empty neighborhoods, passing windowless houses. I am not afraid even though I no longer have the extra weight of my six shooters slapping against my thigh. I'm not worried about the law or anything, and a weird, giddy energy is coursing through me. I'm prepared to travel all night and all day if that's what it takes to get home to my woman.

After a mile or so I realize that I'm still holding the summer sausage. I gnaw off a chunk and appreciate its good salty flavor, but spit it out into the high grass. I put the rest in my saddle bag. I'll save it for Wilma. We'll eat it together. I have no want for food anyway. I want only the comfort that waits for me inside the walls of my own home. Only the tender warmth of female companionship. Only Wilma. Only Wilma.

I Am Still Learning About the World

I slap Matilda on the cheek. Her skin doesn't have much give to it. Still, I know she feels it. She has the right sensors, but she's taking a while to respond. I guess I shouldn't leave her alone for so long, but it's only been two hours. In that time, she got the screws off the electrical panel, and she must have stuck her hand in there, one finger on the hot bar, one to the ground. Her poor knuckles are singed black. There must have been a good-sized spark jumping through her. Lucky it didn't shut her down completely.

I'm still learning about the world, she says.

Yeah, I've heard that before. No matter how realistic she looks, I know she will never be human. She will never be Christine. She won't drink Seven and Seven into the wee hours of the morning, or crank up the stereo and bounce around the kitchen in her underwear, or roll her eyes about the dude who sunbathes next door in his skimpy Speedo, or nudge me awake in the morning, her skin so warm with sleep. No, Matilda is only a very fancy machine and no matter how much I want or wish, she can never be anything but.

I open her shirt and remove the access flap below the frame of her ribs, exposing her main operating components and a scribble of wires. At least her motherboard shows no sign of electric fire. As I push past a wiring harness to inspect her battery, several little sparks leap from her circuitry. They rise like little burning flies but are out before I can pinpoint their origin. Certainly that's not normal. After a minute they stop.

Why did you open the electric panel? I ask.

My cord is lost, so I tried to plug in there. It didn't work.

You need to never do that again.

You are right.

One of these days I'm gonna come home and find you all melted to the floor. I'm serious. Why don't you go upstairs, OK? Put yourself back together. Maybe you can start dinner or something.

OK.

She pulls her skin shut and buttons her shirt. Her footsteps are heavy. Even with the carbon fiber they used to make her frame, she is not as light as you might think. Just look at the dent she has left in my mattress.

I'm still in the basement when I hear glass shattering. Mattie! I shout. What are you doing? I run up the stairs. She is standing in the kitchen with a sparrow in her hand. There is glass all over the counter.

Look at the little chicken, she says.

Let it go. Sit down. Sit down, OK?

What about dinner?

Let the bird go. You're all messed up today, aren't you? We gotta start over. Sit down on this stool, OK?

What about dinner?

Just sit down.

I don't know why they put her reboot button in her armpit. It's such a dumb spot for anything. Granted, she doesn't have sweat glands or ever produce any odor that is remotely offensive. She is only silicon, and plastic, and well-oiled alloys. I run my hand up her shirt, past her somewhat realistic breasts, and under her arm. I press the little button and her eyes flash and she is dead. After a couple seconds, a small whirring sound starts in her chest, and she is alive again. Jack, she says. You're home! Finally, she is herself, my

Matilda 451. She cost me an arm and a leg, all my savings. Everything. Mostly, she's been worth it. It was just so quiet without Christine. The silence was just too much. I couldn't handle it.

Let me get you a beer, Matilda says.

She returns with a cold can and kisses me on the mouth. Her lips are somewhat rigid and a little cold, but I'm used to that. Would you like to lie down before dinner, she says. Without hesitation, she takes my zipper between her burned digits and tugs it open, then awkwardly fishes around in my underwear.

I know I am fucked up for going to bed with her, but her hands feel almost real. I admit, I paid a little extra for this application, along with the "Irish Beauty" upgrade kit. I think it was worth it. I just wanted to feel ribs, spine, shoulder blades, and frankly the breasts were important too. Also, I love her long red hair and how it drops down her back. Still she is not exactly pretty. She's not even a close second to Christine.

It's been over a year since Christine told me I'd better leave, since that night I slept in the backyard under the pine tree, which dripped its miserable sap on me. We were both pretty drunk, and it was sort of a last-straw deal when she found out about what I did with her friend Rita. Oh God. Rita was nothing. Just a mistake. I couldn't even remember, but I'm pretty sure it was true. It was one of those nights when we were all drinking whiskey. Too much whiskey. At least Christine was nice about throwing me out. She's still nice. It makes me miss her more, and it's her that I think of when I'm in bed with Mattie.

Soon it's dark and I am hungry, very hungry, so I announce that we're going out. I'm springing for steaks! She is programmed to seem excited, but it's a super thin expression she wears.

Oh goodie, she says.

She is up and pulling on her fancy underwear, then an old pair of Christine's yoga pants. Somehow those stretchy black leggings ended up in my suitcase. I slept for months with my face nuzzled against the fabric. The faint scent of her was all that sustained me during those hard, lonely days after being kicked out of her life. I do like it when Mattie wears them. In fact, I prefer them.

After I tape some cardboard over the broken window, we head out the back. I hand her the keys, and she positions herself in the driver's seat. There are a series of ports in her stomach region. She lifts her shirt to plug the end of her cable into the GPS. I type in the location and we are on our way. Except for her lead foot, she is pretty decent behind the wheel. This is maybe one of her best features. She is my designated driver.

We pull up in the parking lot behind Bakers Streetcar Bar. There's a large man out there in the alley running a barbeque grill. Oh man, he says, I thought that was Christine for a second. Whoa! Holy Crap!

Hey man, I say, and walk right past him. The steaks smell great and I'm hungry as hell. Everyone stares at us as we enter the bar. Sometimes I forget that Mattie makes sounds as she walks. Each of her movements is connected to some little whirr or click and sometimes even an annoying ping. I pull out a barstool for her. After she's balanced and situated, I order us a round of whiskey and beer. We clink glasses, and I drink, but she only just touches the shot to her lips. Of course liquids cannot enter her mouth. That's a robot no-no. When I'm done with mine, we trade glasses, and I drink hers too.

I hope you like steak, I say.

I am still learning about the world.

Of course you are. This phrase is a factory setting. A disclaimer. I get sick of hearing it, but I don't know how to turn it off.

She continues looking in my direction with her pleasant blank expression. Pretty soon the bartender sets our steaks in front of us. I ignore his weird look. Some people just don't get it. It's not worth trying to explain. I'm starving. I cut into the meat. It's a perfect medium rare. Mattie's too. I watch her slice it into squares and methodically insert it into her mouth. From there it drops into a takeout container, which I can access later.

I'm about halfway through my meal when the door opens and in walks Christine. I feel a cold pang in my temples. I wish I could get off my stool and hug her, but I'm not even sure I can breathe.

Well? she says, standing before us. What's this? I didn't know about this.

This is Mattie, I say, in my best normal voice.

She looks a lot like me.

That's true.

Turning to Mattie, she says, How are the steaks dear?

Oh, they are toothsome.

Toothsome? Huh? Well, I guess I'm going to sit down there with the rest of the real people.

Sure, I say. It's good to see you. Really good.

When I'm done with my steak, I slump in my seat and try to relax. At the other end of the bar, Christine is laughing. The pretty sound of it bounces all around the room. Mattie doesn't really laugh. It's a weird sort of chortle she makes. I order another round. One more shot and one more beer for both of us. I also send a Seven and Seven down to Christine, who hollers her thank you. We toast each other, and Mattie and I clink glasses too.

As it goes, after many drinks, I'm suddenly about to pop. I hate leaving her alone, but I have no choice. I tell Mattie to stay put and don't talk to strangers. This feels like one of the longest trips to the bathroom ever, but I'm only gone for a couple minutes. When I return, Christine is on my stool, and both of the drinks that had been in front of Mattie are empty. A small stream of white smoke is rising from her chest.

Where are your drinks? I say. But Mattie can't answer. She just looks at me and smiles her blank smile. Christine is laughing again.

Oh brother, she says, I don't think your robot can hold her liquor.

What happened?

It was just one shot. Well it was a Car Bomb actually. I showed her how to drop the whiskey in. She seemed to like it.

Oh, no! She's not supposed to have any.

Then why do you bring her to the bar?

There's lots of reasons, I say.

Something in Mattie's chest is hissing. I hear a little pop, and then a larger puff of smoke rises from her shirt. I pay the bill. Cash on the bar. I take Mattie by the shoulder and steer her quickly out the back door. We aren't yet to the middle of the parking lot when her legs freeze up.

Come on Mattie, I say.

I'm still learning about the world, she says, then begins to sputter. Heavy smoke bursts from her mouth. Something in her chest crackles. I have no idea what might make it stop. I go for her reboot button, but her arm is stuck in place and will not let me in. I rip open the back of her shirt and pull forth her takeout container. It's overflowing, and the beer has all run into her central cavity.

I don't know what it means when the smoke turns blue, but it seems like a very bad sign. Then something in her head sparks. I know I need to shut her down. I'm tearing into her shirt, just trying to get to the button in her armpit. But she clamps her elbow against the cage of her ribs. There's just no way. That's when the lid of her head pops open and a small ball of fire shoots high into the air. The flame is white and dazzling; it hangs there in the night. It's a flare. She is calling for help. Sparks continue sputtering from what's left of her head. This is followed by a long deflating sound. I try to catch her, but she is far too heavy, and she burns my hands as she falls. She is totally blown apart. I can't believe it. I paid so much.

That's when the dude from the grill comes out with a five-gallon bucket. Holy fuck, he says. Before I understand what he's doing, he pours it all over her. As the water hits her skin, it turns instantly to steam.

Without her hair she looks terrible. Mattie rolls her head in my direction, trying to focus on me with her pretty glass eyes, then smiles one last time and drops her head on the broken pavement. I have no idea what to do or what can be salvaged. Somehow I know that this is all my fault.

Pretty soon the door opens and Christine comes out. Oh God, she says. What happened?

It's the drinks.

Oh no, I'm so sorry. I really didn't mean to mess her up. Maybe you could take her home and put her in a bag of rice. All we did is one Car Bomb.

She looks at me for a minute, then smiles. You know what they say about us fiery red heads.

I'm not sure what she's getting at. It's not a laughing matter. I'm not going to say it. I'm not going to say anything. I'm broke is all I know. I have nothing to show for it. Nothing at all.

Come on, she says. I'll help.

Really?

Yeah.

She gets Mattie by her armpits. I get her by the legs.

Damn! This girl is so heavy, she says.

Together we load her into the back seat.

I think I might need help getting her out too, I say.

The breeze is catching Christine's hair and flipping it in front of her lips. She rakes it back and looks at me for a long minute, then says, I don't mind helping. It's no problem.

Ripening

It starts in the morning, demanding urgent attention. At first it's kind of great. I mean, I'm human. I like sex, so I do what comes naturally and wrangle the thing into obedience. I'm not thinking there's any issue until a couple minutes later when it's back and maybe just a little bigger, standing straight up in a somewhat superior attitude. So I take care of it once more, but that doesn't work either. After five minutes it's back up, pulsing slightly, radiating heat and redness, telling me the obvious—it has had better friends. It needs one now. It needs Beth.

Well, I have things to do. There is the dog to walk. There is the house to finish painting. I didn't wake up to spend my day dealing with this thing. It's weird because yesterday everything was fine. No issue whatsoever. It just hung around being normal, in mild repose, dangling contently, doing all the things you'd expect a penis to do. Of course, I was getting audited on my liability insurance, and certainly that's nothing to stand up and shout about. But today is different. Today, it has put on some real weight and a little extra height too. I'm not saying this to brag, but after the third round, I can't even button my pants.

Now Darla, my dog, is jumping, standing on her hind legs with her leash in her mouth, ready to water her favorite trees and bushes. I can't blame her. I zip up, best I can, and buckle my belt over it, strapping the darn thing to my belly, then throw on a flannel work shirt that sufficiently hides the bulge.

It's not easy to walk like this. We do a painful lap around the block. The dog is happy as usual to trot ahead of me. She meanders back and forth across the sidewalk, then noses through the shrubbery and sniffs out whatever odors linger in the box elders. I tug on the leash to get her moving. My belt is pinching and pressing, making it hard to swallow.

I wonder about seeing the doctor, but what can they do? Stick a needle in me like last time and inject it with their special shrivel-up medicine. That was terrible and it only worked for an hour. There is no one among their capable staff willing to grab hold of it and ride it into the river.

It's no coincidence that as soon as I'm home, Beth calls. There is something about her that I've never been able to shake. We have known each other forever and are connected in ways that I don't exactly understand. Only thing is, she went and got married. I didn't go to the wedding. No way. In the ten years since, I have not stopped thinking about her or remembering our times together. I just try not to bug her. I'm a decent enough guy. I don't want to mess up her life or anything.

She asks how I am, and I'm not going to lie.

Not so good, I say.

I know. Me neither. My God, I miss you.

Oh shit. I miss you. How's things with Marvin?

The same. I wish I could get out of here.

You can't get out?

Tomorrow I can. Does that work? Are you free?

I can be. Sure.

I told Marv I'm going over to Canada to buy turpentine and then spend the night at my sister's. She'll cover for me. She never liked him anyway.

Darla is barking, so I hang up and shush her. Again, she is asking for something. She sits in front of me panting. I look down at the lump rising from under my shirt, just over my belly. Why can't Beth come over right now? Why do we have to wait until tomorrow? I'm suffering, and I know, in her own way, she is too. I open a tin of smoked oysters and eat them all. I make scrambled eggs, a half dozen, and devour them too. Cleaning up the pan, I get to thinking. Somehow I can't remember the exact spot where we're supposed to meet. I need to call her back, but I'm nervous about Marvin answering. My brain is muddy for sure. I have fallen on hard times. I could say that. Hard times are here. I laugh at my own joke. There is nothing to do but wait for tomorrow. After several painfully slow hours, I cinch my belt, strapping my very difficult, very tiresome penis tight to my belly, and go for supplies. I'll need sour cream donuts, a dozen of them; cigarettes and whiskey; and a couple more tins of smoked oysters. I need to get drunk.

TOMORROW TAKES FOREVER, but finally it's here. My condition has worsened. I suffer through the afternoon and finally, around five, I throw on a long coat and head for the river. I'm maybe a little early. I'm just so eager to see Beth. I'm not a creep. I did not come here to leer at anyone or make anyone uncomfortable, especially the young couple who keep kissing. They look so fresh and pink-skinned and sick with love. They are lucky. If I spend too long looking at them, it's purely an accident. The ugly truth of my situation is that there is a thick stalk of flesh rising from between my legs. It has grown out of control, but I didn't come here to show it to anyone. Just Beth. It's only for her.

I open my lawn chair and sit down. Only it seems that there is no longer any comfortable position for me. This penis has become an irritating truss, now pressing at me, just above my navel.

Waiting for Beth is impossible. I don't know what's keeping her, but this whole thing is driving me crazy. As I stare out over the canal, the water dimples and stirs. I know the river is thick with carp. I'm not crazy about going in there. I don't know if those things bite, but they're just so big and stupid and only want one thing, and that's to eat. As far as I'm concerned, they can just keep filling their bellies with pollution from the treatment plant, and let their blood turn to dirt. Just don't eat me or come anywhere near my penis.

It's almost dark. It would just be nice if we can make this happen so I can at least get some decent rest.

I twist the lid from a tin of smoked oysters. I remember how Beth loves them. I love them too. I sip whiskey. Then before I know it, I have stupidly eaten all the oysters. I am also a little drunk. I cannot wait any longer. This thing is making me crazy. I undress to my swim trunks, which don't even come close to containing me. It's an ugly sight, I'm sure. With no one here to see, it doesn't matter. I walk quickly to the water and don't stop until I'm chest deep. Again I wait. Leaking pale ribbons into the slow current. Worrying that the carp with their hard-lipped mouths will sniff me out and come nibbling.

Where the hell is Beth? I hope to God I didn't mix up the plan. I thought we agreed this was the place. Maybe I should have called her. I never did call. She always calls me. I can't call. I am not drunk enough to handle this sort of disappointment. By the time I get out, my fingers are tingling, my toes too. The ugly truth is while I was in the canal, it grew again, and now rises to a point just below my ribs. A gnarled post of flesh. It feels like it may burst, like it will simply explode, leaving a huge crater in the ground. Finally, I give up. It's the worst thing not seeing Beth. I'm sure it's just as bad for her too. Something must be wrong.

I PANIC AT my own door. My landline is ringing. It's Beth of course. She's calling. I flip the lock and run through the house in a flailing motion, penis bouncing under my shirt, aching all down between my legs. I grab for the phone. Beth!

Where were you? she whispers in the phone.

I tell her exactly where I waited, and waited and waited.

I was at the lagoon, she said. I thought we had it all worked out. I was there for hours and you never came and you didn't text or anything.

I thought you told me landlines only.

I did, she says.

Well, I was at the river. You said the river. So I went to our spot. Same spot as last year.

I said the lagoon. The lagoon is better. There's no one there.

Oh my God. Yes. I remember now. I don't know how I fucked it up. I'm not thinking straight. Can't we just drive there right now?

Obviously not. No. We can't. I just can't. Marvin will know for sure.

How are you? Are you OK?

No. I'm not OK. I'm sore. I'm dying here, she says. I'm so swollen. It's worse than last year. The lips are just getting thicker and thicker, and so sensitive. I can't handle it, but also I can't stop touching it. It's making me crazy, all flipped apart and gaping, feeling so empty and lost, wanting everything to be shoved inside. I'm serious. My dildos aren't working anymore. They're too small. I'm looking at a lamp right now, just the base of it. Thinking of how that would feel. A lamp! It's crazy, but the shape is nice, so tall and thick. I could probably make it work if I took it apart, got rid of the bulb and switch, so there was just that smooth tall ceramic base. That's what's happening here. You understand? I'm going nuts. Oh God! Of course, it's made a terrible mess out of my underwear. I can't wear them anymore, pants either. I soak them in like five minutes. I'm a mess. I'm fucking disaster. I need you inside me. Like right now!

Just hearing her say so is about the sweetest, most amazing thing ever. The words go right to my penis, to its already over-inflated head. Right then it adds another inch. More pain, more ache.

Same thing, I say. I'm dying too. Absolutely dying. Well, can you? Can you get out?

I told you I can't. Marvin will know.

How can he not know already?

I don't know, but he doesn't.

I don't have any clue how Marvin could sleep through her time of need, but I'm so glad he does. She and I have a deep connection. Deeper than any marriage vow. I love her—in heart, in soul, but mostly in body. We are tangled together by vein, by artery, and by blood that beats from a single heart, full of pain and desire. Her pain is my pain. Mine is hers.

BEFORE I HANG up, we explicitly, very clearly, nail down the spot and time for the following day, reviewing it several times. Only problem is that tomorrow is forever away. I begin drinking. I have a bottle of whiskey. It's helpful but I only seem to drift in and out of sleep. Mostly, I just lie in my bed, feeling the intense throbbing of my penis. This thing has taken on the weight of an arm. I don't know how much blood is required to fill it, but it must be a lot. Drunk or not, it scares me. It's up just beyond my nipples. How can I sleep with this thing lying its weight across my chest, throbbing ridiculously? I am afraid to give it the exercise it demands. I'm afraid of what will come out of it.

Hours later, I wake. The room smells like the saltiest ocean. I find my penis is balanced at the window, leaning its head on the glass, looking somewhat wistful. Well, this is a new development. Actually I feel much better without it attached. It stands very still, heaving slightly, balanced on its balls. The windowsill is shining with tears. It is crying.

I check the clock. It's 4 a.m., the dead of night. From the absolute quiet, the phone rings. I am ecstatic. Maybe she has changed her mind. I throw off the covers. Maybe this is it. Maybe she has figured a way to sneak out, and we can take care of everything, once and for all. I leap for the phone to catch her before she changes her mind or hangs up. What I don't realize is how slippery the floor has become. The entire room is skinned with a glistening liquid. Halfway across the room, my feet shoot out from under me. I land on my back with a walloping blow, slamming my head on the hardwood. I can barely see for the stars bursting in the air. Oh no! I am missing the call. No! The dog is licking my face with her large, warm tongue. I lie on the floor and listen to the far-off sound of the answering machine. It is Beth. She's talking about now. About right now! That's when I see that the door has opened. It shuts quickly with a slam that rattles all the windows. My penis is gone.

MY HEAD THROBS. A large egg has risen on the back of my skull. I stand and look down at the loose sleeve of skin hanging from my groin. It's not so pretty. I fold it over and keep moving. Honestly, I am relieved to be rid of the thing, but also afraid of what it might do. I call her. She should answer. Please answer. All her phone does is ring and ring. I pull on my jeans and throw on a hoodie. I'm out the door, jumping in my car. Driving through the steam clouds of the incinerator. I go right to the river.

I'M NOT SURPRISED to find her at the lagoon, sitting in a patch of grass.

It's about time, she says.

The water is churning just past the lily pads. Dim streaks of flesh surface, then recede and rise again. It's bizarre and grotesque, but somehow beautiful too. Small waves ring the activity and roll slowly past the lilies and cattails, breaking at the shore with a light slap. I'm filled with a huge sense of relief. That's us out there. We have slipped out together and created one of the weirdest things you'd ever see. I think that's her uterus, pulsing and shining with tubes that run from either side of it, ending in large flowers of tissue. The vagina is thick and swollen all the way down to the ruffled skirting of the vulva. It's a strange and wonderful costume that my penis has wriggled into.

I tried to call you, she says. It couldn't wait.

I know.

It left without me.

Mine too.

What are we going to do? she says.

Wait it out. Deal with it.

I guess, she says.

Feel this, I say. I direct her hand to the bump on my head.

Ouch. Are you OK?

Better now that I'm here. For sure, I'm better. I'll just be glad when it's all done.

It won't be long now, she says. I'm already a little sad, thinking about tomorrow, wishing things could be different.

She is right. The next morning we will be ourselves again. Everything will be as it was. I'll be wilted between my legs, a nothing-special sex organ, and she'll be put back too. I'm sure we'll both feel a little guilty, but also relieved. I know I'll miss her terribly. I'll obsess for months. But neither of us will call or write the other. This is just how it goes.

At least now and for the next hour, we are together. There is nothing in the world that we need to do but wait. I put my arms around her shoulder and rest my cheek against hers, giving her the smallest kiss. With the moon behind the clouds, it's hard to see, but I can tell from the growing sound of the waves slapping the shore that it's about to be finished. I know what she's thinking. I feel it too. Nothing matters but this moment. We are together. Lying in the grass, holding on to each other, waiting.

Her Walls Not Mine

I haven't left my apartment in almost a month. The pain is still pretty damn startling. If I shift wrong, it can absolutely knock me on my ass. It's bad shit. The saving grace is that I'm OK sitting still, drinking beer is not a problem, and the weed I smoke is prescription strength. It's no wonder my belly has gone to blubber. The work of all those sit-ups is totally wasted. Where are the veins that once popped on my biceps and webbed my forearms? Gone!

I spend the morning propped on pillows in front of the tube, thumbs sore from the video game controller. I have gotten real good at running through the cartoon world with all its angular canyons. Watch as I fuck up the bad guys, with their turbans and orange beards and squinty Osama Bin Laden eyes. Boom! I shoot fireballs and hollow-point bullets, set bombs, and blow the crap out of the fortress wall. Bricks fly everywhere and I move on to the next level. It's exhausting. It takes all my willpower to toss the controller aside and flick off the TV. Without it going, the world is dead quiet. It's unsettling, till at last a car rips down my street, motor roaring zero to fifty on this quarter-mile neighborhood block.

Upstairs there is Felice in her own apartment. I wonder if she is traipsing around in her underwear or less. I listen for the patter of her nice little feet, but there is nothing. Sometimes this place feels so big and empty. I clench, I crunch, and then drag my sorry body through the kitchen to the small window in the pantry and brace myself against the shelves. From here I can see into the back-yard and confirm what I suspected. Her car is gone. Without it, the grass looks high and wild. Some crazy-ass vine with large leaves and gaudy purple flowers loops through the chain link.

Beyond the fence there is the alley that flanks all our yards. My neighbor in the house opposite mine is standing shirtless at his grill, his giant stomach propped on thin, hairless legs. His skin is bright with sunburn. He flips sausage with his fingers, recoiling from the hot grease. I watch as his wife throws open the door, wearing only a flimsy night thing. She is a sturdy woman, round and busty, with black hair and blood-red lipstick. Her stomach has a similar girth to his. She shouts some directive, but it doesn't seem to have any impact on him. She turns and spits into the mums. I've seen these two at night, walking naked past their windows. Nudists, I guess. I told Felice about it but she didn't believe me.

Those people? Oh God! she said. I can't picture that.

It's true, I said. I wonder how do they do it, you know? I mean they're both so damn fat. How do they get the parts together?

You would wonder, she said.

I got nothing to do but wonder, I said. This is the weirdest place I've ever lived.

I HAVE A slab of ribs in marinade, ready to go. I get the fire going on my own grill. I keep it right here on the front porch. I know the neighbors aren't so crazy about me barbequing out here, so I keep the flame low as I can. It's best when it drops between the coals and glows. I got my spray bottle just in case. I have a decent chair, too, that's got plenty of pillow. So it's no problem to hang out there a good portion of the afternoon, turning the meat, brushing it with hot sauce.

One nice thing about living here—all our porches line up, all down the street. We can all sit out here, pass joints if we want and talk to one another. Only a bunch of my neighbors don't speak English or smoke weed or even drink beers. Then there are the new Arabic people across the street. They moved into Joe's old place and built a tall fence around the house, which throws off the whole neighborly, porch-sitting thing. That's the first thing about them. Then the women wear all black, every day. Like they gotta disappear. I've seen four of them. Every bit of them covered. No skin whatsoever. No neck or arms or leg to speak of. Only eyes and some don't even show those. Live and let live, I say. But the damn fence kills me. One dude lives there with three or four women, sons galore, and a decent car too, a Range Rover. Must be nice, having all that extra pussy under one roof.

FINALLY FELICE IS home, just back from her class or wherever. God bless her. She carries a thirty-pack of cheap beers.

You doing alright today? she asks.

Oh yeah, always a little better each day, I say.

You want a beer? she asks. It's happy hour somewhere.

Sure is, I say. I'll take one.

She pulls one from the box. It's finally Friday, she says.

Is it really? Holy shit! My days are all glommed together. You got time to sit and sip a couple with me? I'm making ribs, if you want some.

They do smell good. Give me a minute. I'll be back, she says, then bounces upstairs.

I listen as her footsteps vanish into the house. They are light and quick. She moves like a little rabbit, hopping around up there. Her floor barely creaks. I got a little too much time on my hands. I know it's pathetic the way I listen for her movements, guessing at what she's up to. Noticing the sound of her plumbing, the kitchen sink, the tub and toilet. Waiting to hear her small feet cascade down the stairs in her usual zippy manner. Just once I wish she would invite me up.

I'm not sure what inspired my neighbor Brent to go cranking up the stereo in his custom van. He has Anita Baker singing "Sweet Love" or some such gunk. He proceeds to polish his tires and bumpers. Without a belt, his pants don't have much of a grab at his waist, and he shows a good deal of butt crack as he bends, shining up the black rubber. He owns the house next to the new fence. He's been there about a year. I wasn't sure about him at first. One thing is, he can't talk right. Words stumble from his mouth, making only bits and pieces of sense. Another thing is that he spends a lot of time sweeping the sidewalk, the street, even his grass. I heard he was in a car accident. Smashed his head. Joggled his brain.

Fence, he says, shaking his head, tall, damn.

Yeah, I say. It's big. Sure is. Big fence. Hmm.

He stands looking confused. Party man, he says, pointing to the beer in my hand. Twelve-pack, party. Yeah?

No party here, I say. Just hanging out. This is my medicine, I say. That's different.

Girl, nice, blonde hair, blonde hair. Girl. Your wifely?

She's not, I say. She just lives upstairs.

Not your wifely? He looks confused, then holds up his spray bottle and offers to polish the wheels on my Chevy.

Sure, I say. Go at it.

Again, I am wondering what it would be like to lie side by side with Felice. What would I hear then? The sound of food walking around her stomach. Truly I'm injured, but the important parts still work pretty darn good. Maybe too good. At last, Felice zips down the stairs with more beers.

It's so awesome out today. I love October, she says. And now, I'm done with all my crap for the day so I can focus on my drinking.

Good plan, I say.

She pulls her chair near mine and cracks open the beers.

Across the street, four men, all in black, including the dude who owns the place, exit the fence and stand flat-footed on the sidewalk, smoking and looking dismal. Hmm, she says, they don't seem like they're having much fun. Meanwhile Brent keeps Anita Baker cranked, still showing his butt crack and bobbing his head as he wipes another neighbor's tires. I turn to Felice.

How many wives do you think he's got? You think he has more than one?

Shoot, she says. I don't know. I've seen more than one in the yard. Who knows? They barely come out.

Then like five boys burst from the gate, all wearing little suits, and climb into their dad's Range Rover. One has the key and proceeds to start the engine then begins honking the horn. Finally, their father snaps. Stop it! Turn it off! He wears a haggard look. I'm not sure what's going on with him. Maybe all his wives are withholding.

Pretty soon more men arrive carrying big trays of steaming food. More wives too, draped in black.

Maybe it's some sort of holiday, Felice says. Well, I'm gonna go find out. With a beer in hand she strolls across the street, her blonde hair flipping in the breeze. They talk for a while, until she is also shaking her head and looking somewhat stunned. Returning, she is almost picked off by an ice cream truck. Jeez, she says, climbing the porch. They're going to a wake. Their brother was murdered.

Are you kidding? That sucks.

Yeah, she says, he was a clerk at a convenience store. They shot him and robbed him. He has a wife and kid too. They are still over in Yemen.

What a shit deal, I say.

Yeah, he moved here to get out of Yemen because of the fighting, and was only trying to raise enough money to get his wife and kid out of there too. It's such a crappy irony.

God damn.

You want me to get you another beer? she asks. I think I'm out.

Sure, I say. It makes the medicine go down even better.

While she's gone a boy in a suit emerges from the fence, carrying two plates of food. He crosses the street and climbs our porch.

What's this for? I ask.

It's for you, he says.

What for?

The boy shrugs and runs back home and disappears through the gate.

I don't know what I've done to deserve anything from these people. I peel back the tinfoil. The first plate is filled with triangular fritters that remind me of wontons. They're crunchy and full of ground beef. Perfect beer-drinking food. The second plate is heaped with rice and chicken, potato, and zucchini. There is also flat bread folded in and filled with honey. When Felice comes back with the beers, I tell her we've got dinner and more dinner.

Are you kidding? What's going on?

Check it out. I pull the foil and show her the food.

That's amazing, she says.

She carries everything upstairs, including the ribs. Then comes back for me. It takes us a good couple minutes to manage the steps, and it damn about kills me, but she has her arm around me and we take it one step at a time. When I finally make it to her kitchen, I'm about to pass out. I gulp. I gasp. I ease into a chair. God, I am grateful to be here. It's a nice place, way better than mine. I'm surprised to see she has pom-poms hanging on the wall, over a shelf of small trophies too.

Were you a cheerleader or something? I ask.

Yeah, in high school, and a little in college too. It was like an extension of gymnastics. It kept me in shape. Plus I love sports.

Oh yeah, me too, I say. Did you date the captain of the football team?

Actually, my twin sister did. She gets everything she wants. Still does. You look like you did sports.

I did, I say, football and soccer. Now I just play video games. I'm bulking up.

Felice sets the table, opens more beers, and we take our time eating.

The samboosas are really good, she says, your pork ribs too.

Soon, I am stuffed, and in a pleasant digestive stupor, I gaze out her window into the neighbors' home. It's astonishing how close these houses are. As I watch the lady comes into view, her baby sleeping on her shoulder. She leans slowly over the crib to put it to bed, but the kid throws its arms back and screams, just realizing the most awful thing is about to happen.

Yeah, Felice says, poor Mom is trying to get a break from her little beast.

The baby screams so loud we can hear it through the walls.

It's really a sweet baby, Felice says. I've held it before, very sweet.

She carries the dinner plates through the dark and sets them on the counter, then opens her porch door.

Oh my gosh, it's true! she says. You were right. Do you see them?

Oh yeah, I say.

Oh God! she says, I love it!

Across the alley, our nudist neighbors are passing the open windows. They talk, smoke, drink, and scratch their bellies. He ties a trash bag. Then opens the rear door and tosses it outside into the open air. His penis bobs. Ridiculous.

Do you ever walk around here without your clothes? I ask. I mean with the shades open?

I guess sometimes I do, she says, but not on purpose, and not to be a nudist, but just because I'm busy and it doesn't always matter. I have seen the neighbors next door, just once, by accident. It was sort of an ordinary, nothing special deal. Not like those people across the alley. I'm pretty sure they know everyone can see them and they're doing it on purpose, like to prove something. I mean who takes out trash in the buff? Maybe it's their dinner routine. Maybe they are getting ready to sit down and eat hamburgers. Or maybe they are working up to sex. Maybe this is the foreplay to their fore-play. I can't imagine.

After a minute she leans across the table. Her face is serious, and I think she might kiss me, but she only asks how long before I'm all better.

I really don't know, I say. I think it's going to be a while.

She tightens her lips. But you are going to get better, aren't you?

I am, I say. For sure.

Since the sun has set, the darkness has gathered all around us, and she hasn't done anything to stop it.

That's good, she says.

I keep expecting her to stand and tell me it's time for me to leave. Like maybe she has a date to get to or something. But so far she's not kicking me out. After a bit, I extract a joint that I rolled earlier. I light it for her. The weed is strong and good, but just being here, in this chair in her kitchen, surrounded by her walls, not mine—that is the best medicine.

When Drink, Drugs, and Floor Polish Steal Your Youth and Trash Your Woman

OF course the fish are dead. They dried up and curled at the tail. Fish need water. I've tried to explain this to her. I don't know why I bother. I'm talking to the wall here. And she looks at me like I just kicked her in the shin, but I didn't touch her. I maybe bumped her ankle earlier with my wheelchair and that probably left a bruise, but that was an accident. She takes an armful of my laundry and crams it in the dresser. There's no good reason to be mad at me just because I'm trying to make a point.

She forgets stuff. First she forgets how Martinez turned her out and how I let her come back, and then she forgets how I saved her. Sometimes I think I shouldn't have. I sure as shit wouldn't be so messed up now. That was the night she poured that floor polish into a cup and drank it right in front of me. Out of spite. She would have swallowed more if I didn't slap it from her hand. It made her shake and flip around the floor. Her arms bent up like a praying mantis. I tried dragging her to the car, but it was impossible with her jerking around like she did. Finally, I called the ambulance, which was smart because I was loaded too.

Two days later she blinked awake out of the coma. Two more days and she came home to fill the house with the sharp smell of her stomach. She is sick still, brainsick. But for some reason God wanted to make her better. I guess he wouldn't let her die—not until she finished the hard work of ruining my life.

55

I'm in this wheelchair now because I let her drive. We were coming home from Martinez's. My old friend Martinez is up on Seven Mile. He's the guy with the good stuff. So, she had the wheel and she was killing my buzz, arguing about something and going too fast through nowhere Detroit, just not looking at anything and pointing her finger at me. Truth is I wasn't paying attention either, until she hopped the curb and then slammed the telephone pole. That's when my femur snapped like a carrot. Metal hammered into my leg and my ankle ground up like blender ice. Bones popped out of my skin. Bloody Mary. Dirty Harry, I said, and then I passed out.

I got a room at the hospital. They set me up with a foxy nurse. She had a tattoo of a lady's face on her neck. She was the bearer of some very good medicines too, not as good as Martinez's but better when you double them up. After a four-week stay, they sent me home with a goodie bag full of pills, and ten pages of instructions in print too small to read.

I'm getting better still, but it's been some months since I worked, doing my job at the transfer station, and then I had to have surgery and then the infection happened because who-knows-why, and then more surgery. At least they didn't take off my leg and toss it in the scrap pile. One day, they say, I might be able to walk again, only I don't know. Below my knee, the thing is all swollen up like a watermelon. It doesn't look like a leg at all.

It's snowing out tonight and I wonder how long this winter can last. It's been forever already, living in gloom. The snow is all cold and bad and tumbling out of the sky and sticking on the cars and streetlights, putting its sick freeze on the world.

She wheels me to the kitchen in time to grab the phone. I'm just sitting there listening to the radio, waiting for her to hang up. She puts it to my ear so I can hear. It's the electric company's computer again, calling to say they are going to shut us off.

Bastards! she says. What the hell are we going to do without power?

Light candles, I guess.

We'll freeze, stupid!

She opens the fridge and pulls out some beers. We sit at the table and look at each other. The radio is playing a good Led Zeppelin song. When it's over, the announcer starts yammering about Kwame.

Oh shit, did you hear about this, she says. The fucking mayor is in jail. That one on Conant. Hah! I hope they leave him there forever. Lying bastard.

What do you have against him? He's not the one turning off our power. You don't even know him.

I know he's a fucking liar.

She's rubbing her hands together. Making a sound like sandpaper. Where's my lotion, she says.

I point to the TV.

How did it get behind the TV? she asks.

I don't know, I say. Why does anything get behind the TV?

That's around the time somebody starts pounding on our front door. We're not expecting anyone. I guess it shouldn't have been a surprise. None of it should have been. But bad news always is.

She looks at me and scowls. After we hear the feet tromp back down the steps and the car roar away, she goes to check the porch, returning with an official-looking paper surrounded by wide swaths of blue tape. It's a bad joke signed by a judge. It declares eviction. She throws it in my lap.

I guess we don't have to worry about our power getting shut off anymore, she says.

What am I supposed to do with this? I ask. I wad it up and throw it at her as she walks from the room. Mostly, I'm ready for another beer. I can almost get one on my own, but she intentionally keeps them way in back where I can't reach from my chair.

I wheel into the bedroom and ask her to get me another can. She's in the closet emptying her clothes from the rod and dropping them on the floor. I work myself into the bed using the railing and my one good leg. I can do it, just barely.

What are you doing? I ask

Packing.

Why?

Didn't you hear? she says. The bastard bank is taking the house, baby. We have to go.

Leaving seems ridiculous. The whole building is filled with our stuff. It's huge. Two stories tall with a basement and an attic. We can't move. It's impossible.

Call the fucking DHS, I say. It's inhumane. They can't throw us out. It's snowing.

The DHS isn't going to do shit.

It's funny then because she's found the big bottle of whiskey that I stashed in the back of the closet, just before the accident. I forgot about it. Holy shit. Happy day! She undoes the screw top, upends it and guzzles a good amount.

Hey, let me have some, I say. You share with me—I share with you.

Shut up, she says. You don't share.

There is some truth to that. I know. It's getting late. She sits on the bed with me, and we take turns with the bottle. Already my stomach is hurting, so I chase it with antacid. After a while she pulls off her clothes until she's wearing nothing but her bruises.

Where's my fucking underwear? she asks.

How could you lose them? Check the floor, I say. Check behind the TV. How about the fishbowl. Oh that's right. That's where the dead fish live. I close my eyes and listen to her flat feet banging around the room.

Then she is pouring more booze into my throat.

Thank you, I say, and I mean it. I am grateful. She settles back into bed and we drink more. I look over at her and wonder if she is turning orange or is it just the bad light. What are we eating to make that happen? Her lips are as chapped as her face.

What are we going to do, sweetie? she says, her voice softer now.

I don't know. Go to your aunt's place. Go to Martinez's. Find a shelter.

I'm not staying in one of those places. There's no way.

No fucking way.

After a while she says, I want to fuck one last time in this crappy old house.

That sounds alright, I guess, as long as she's careful about my leg. But first we need these special fuck pills. I have a couple more that I got from Martinez. I take one and wait for something to happen.

I don't think it's going to work, I say. My dick is too drunk.

We lay next to one another. Me with my hand in the kink of hairs between her legs. I don't want to look at her. I just want to lie there. I want to remember how she used to be. I try but all I can think of is that nurse with the tattoo on her neck. Something about her reminded me of the circus. I used to try and dream about her. I'd sleep with my hand between my legs and think of her mouth and all the great things it might say if she let it.

Now my woman's got me in her rough fingers and is flipping me all around, but it's not working. After a while she swears quietly and gives up. My dick is just a useless flap of skin.

Remember that time with the gasoline? she says. She's smiling and glowing with whiskey.

That was funny as shit.

You didn't have any sense then either, she says.

It's only that we were out of lighter fluid, so we used gasoline and dumped it all over the charcoal. The fire exploded. It flashed a bright pop and shocked the air and an orange fireball rolled up the backside of the house. It was like a little bomb went off. The air shuddered and we stood there with our salt shaker and our meat on a plastic plate and our beers and watched the siding curl and twist, stunned that something so stupid was happening right in front of us. Instead of trying to fix it, I kept thinking how I needed to start over and try that again, and this time not fuck it up, and probably just move the grill a little further from the building. Who cares about the mulberry tree anyway? Not me.

The blackest, foulest smoke rose into the sky and got pushed back down between the houses and spun all around us.

Get the hose! she yelled, and then smacked me in the head. I started running, only I couldn't get the thing to thread on the bib. I turned the water on and it blew off the pipe. She was standing in the grass next to the gas can and yelling to hurry. My skin was pink and burned some. The hair on my arms had shriveled down to kinks. I was trying to get the threads to line up and make the hose work when she said, Oh fuck it. Forget it.

When I finally looked back up, I saw the siding had melted to stringy plastic, and the fire had burned itself out. She was laughing her ass off. We were OK. We didn't burn up our house or the neighbors, but I didn't start laughing until I realized it had singed her eyebrows into dark little stubs. Oh, shit. That was a good day. We grilled our meat, and drank ourselves to perfection, and my dick still worked that night when she got hold of it. It worked fine. That was one of the last times.

She touches me now, still trying to get the thing to stand. I never meant to end up like this, unshowered and bad smelling, with a watermelon foot. My woman unable to make my dick work.

Relax, she says.

How can I? We have two days before the Bailiff comes with the cops or whoever. Before they throw us in the street. Or before I shoot them all in the head.

We should just torch the place, she says. We should.

Damn right.

I'm not kidding.

I'm not either. I'd burn it right to the ground before I give it to those assholes.

She kisses me, which is a surprise, because when was the last time she did that? It's been forever. And I know I'm onto something. My heart beats with the idea. It's pounding hard with steady, even thumps. It feels right, and somehow this talk of burning our life to the ground has got me feeling young again.

I know just where that gas can is. It hasn't moved in months from its spot next to the garage door. We're only two blocks from the service station. Who cares what it looks like, my old lady filling up her container so late at night, with snow falling everywhere. Carrying it home in a laundry bag. It's not illegal to buy gasoline.

Fuck those bastards, she says.

I can see a happiness swirling in her eyes. She is kissing me. There is a wild heat in her mouth. Her tongue is a flame. She touches it to mine and for the first time in months, she sets me alive, she gets me burning, and I'm filling with heat and blood, and standing up. God damn it—I'm standing up. I'm ready for her.

Come on baby, I say. Come on.

Dexter's Song

It was one of those cool tunes that stuck with you and made you think ahead, and just ride on the notes. I probably was rushing the theme a little, but I didn't feel meter quite like Dexter. His sense of beat was balls-on perfect.

Slow down, man, he said.

I tried, but mostly I liked to drop my head and disappear into the song. So maybe I hit it a little too hard, and maybe lost track of myself, but that's how I play best.

We kept at it for another hour, but by three thirty, my attention was beginning to switch to the dull need rising in my chest. Dex wasn't stupid. I know he sensed my urgency.

Let's do it again tomorrow, he said. I think we can stretch the song some. We can make it last all afternoon if we want.

Yeah, maybe, I said.

I pulled my sax apart, and wiped it down, and stuck it in its case.

Sure, I was in a hurry to get to my doctor's house. Only today I screwed up, and when I stood, my case split open and my horn dropped to the concrete floor with a loud clang. I scooped it up quick but the damage was done. My dumb move left a ding in the brass bell, tweaked my octave key, and bent a couple of the uppers too. The pads barely hit the holes. I reassembled it and tried some notes. The sound was all airy and wrong. Damn, I said. I did a number on it this time.

Bend it back, man.

I'm not even sure it's fixable.

C'mon.

I shook my head. I'm serious, I said. It's bad.

WITH NOTHING BETTER to do than beat myself in the head, I rode my bike as fast as I could over to Bullet's and bought a bindle of *Horse Head*. The small paper wrap was folded into an origami with an ink stamp of a horse. I snorted a pinch in his living room, and finally feeling halfway decent for the first time that day, I thanked Dr. Bullet, got back on my bike, and pedaled real slow down Cass. Even though it was only November, little bits of snow had started falling and gradually were turning into something heavier and beginning to build up in the streets. Pretty soon everything was slippery as hell, and cars could no longer drive but only go skidding down the road.

Still very bummed about trashing my sax, I chained up my bike and walked into the Cass Café. There was a crowd, for a Tuesday, and all the seats were taken, so I wedged myself in at the bar and ordered a Stroh's.

I emptied the can and was about to get another when the girl next to me gave a little nudge with her elbow. I think I saw you play at Bert's a couple weeks ago. Am I right? Saxophone?

Yeah. That was me. What did you think?

Good. Real good, she said. I'm serious.

Thanks.

My ex was a musician, she said. I used to go with him to Bert's every Wednesday. Drove me a little crazy, but saw some great music. I still hit it every so often. Whenever I'm sure he's not going to be there.

I told her about the messed-up problem with my sax, and turning toward me, she pushed the last bit of a ketchup-coated hamburger into her mouth, chewed and nodded, and then said she might actually have one that I could borrow.

Really. Are you kidding?

Do I kid? she said, turning to her friend for backup.

No, Sabrina doesn't kid. Even when she's drunk.

That's most of the time, Sabrina said. So yeah. For real.

Only the days of the week that end with y, her friend said.

How much are you looking for? I asked.

I don't know. Maybe we could figure a trade or something. It's a pretty nice horn.

The windows of the café were fogged. There's nothing out there in the dark worth looking at anyway. But in here, all these ideas are getting talked out, riding on warm breath. That's what's condensing on the glass. That's why I like it here.

You ready to go?

Yeah, her friend said, Let's get out of here.

Sabrina opened her purse and gave me her card. Call me if you want the sax, she said.

As the two left, walking into the snow, I stood at the bar, turning her card over in my hand. Flowers surrounded the cursive letters of her name. In the lower corner above her phone number it read, For all occasions.

THE FOLLOWING SATURDAY, I rode my bike way the hell up Woodward, past Maple, through inhospitable traffic. Finally turning into her neighborhood, my heart beating fast from all those damn cars ripping around me, I pedaled down her street with its tall stone houses, amazed at the smoothness of the cement. As far as I could see, there were no broken or dead trees anywhere.

There you are, she said. I gave up on you.

She was standing on her brick driveway, wearing a small red coat, holding a drink in her hand.

It's a hell of a ride out here.

C'mon, she said.

I walked my bike into her garage and leaned it up next to her sweet car. She led me into the house, explaining about how she moved back here after her divorce and how her parents were still at their lake house.

Just throw your coat anywhere, she said. I'm drinking gin today. You want some?

I need some water. I'm gonna die if I drink gin.

Alright.

She ran the tap, then poured herself another from a tall blue bottle. That was when I noticed the saxophone leaned up in the corner of the living room.

That's the horn?

That's it.

Cool. Are you serious. It's a Selmer.

Yep. It's Lars's. My ex. Fuck him.

He doesn't want it?

I don't give a shit if he does. It's mine now. We're divorced and it's still here in my house.

How much you want for it?

I don't know. Just borrow it.

Really?

It's OK with me.

Holy hell, what a sweet horn it was. She obviously had no idea it was worth some real dough. I changed the reed and tried a scale. The sound was so warm compared to my old busted axe, with its bell full of dents, and pads duct-taped into place.

After I got the brass warmed up, I played the crazy song that Dexter had written. The tone was so round and rich and dark and the action of the valves so sweet. Looking at Sabrina, I could see that something amazing had just happened.

Damn, she said, You're really really good. So much better than my ex ever was. Sounds like Coltrane in here, she said. Like something off *Love Supreme*.

I don't know about that.

Sounds so good. Really, I'm serious.

It's a damn fine horn.

How about I make you a drink now?

She toasted me and finished hers.

OK, just one. Then I gotta split. I got practice to get to.

She hit the fridge door and ice shot out. Then she dumped in some gin, poured in some bubbles too.

Here you are.

After we clinked, she took me by the neck and kissed me on the mouth. Her tongue was pretty sour for a rich girl. I guess I expected something else.

She led me into the next room and tried to get me to sit on the big white furry rug, lamb's wool or something, right there in front of the fireplace. Logs popped and hissed, and she took off her sweater and kissed me more. The whole thing felt like a setup. I mean when does anything this good ever happen to me. Did I step out of my life and into some dumb movie? All I could think was this girl's trouble. I knew I should not sprawl on her damn animal rug or get too comfortable anywhere in this house. It felt like any moment the police might barrel through the door and arrest me. No doubt, I was on the wrong side of Eight Mile. I wished I'd at least brought a bindle, but was too nervous about cops, and nice as Sabrina looked, I told her I had to split.

POOR FUCKED UP Bullet, with all his titanium plates and stainless screws. He couldn't lift his arm over his chest, and his legs popped and cracked when he walked, but his smack was always good. He lived near Seven Mile, up where the Grand Trunk crossed and the buildings were filled with bricks and tires and no longer needed every I-beam to hold them up. Since winter hadn't really taken hold yet, I spent a lot of time with his torch kit, burning beams out of a pretty decent three-story warehouse. I was the first scrapper to hit it, so I had my pick of copper and steel too. Still, and always, the work was dirty and got old quick. My hands stiffened and my legs were so sore from the combination of the cold and the demands of hauling all that heavy material. It was a crappy job, harvesting this shit. Dangerous too, with wide-open elevator shafts gaping in dark corners of the building, waiting to swallow me and break every one of my bones. Despite the rotten work, the cash payout at the scrapyard was immediate and kept me in the dope.

During the second half of December, the freeze came and it was terrible. It was getting real hard to live without heat. I kept in touch with Sabrina. I even had her over a couple times, and she said she loved my place—I can't say why. It was my parents' from years back. They rented it out for a while; then tiring of the hassle, they gave it to me. It's over near the City Airport, and all summer it had grown crazy with vines that grabbed for the walls and wedged between the boards and crawled inside the stud bays, shooting weird yellow leaves under the base moldings. But nothing about winter, with its mud and cold, was so romantic, and I got real tired of riding my bike to the gas station, just to keep the lights on and space heaters glowing. The constant annoying roar of the generator built up too, making for a long, dull headache. Then my pipes froze, and one popped and spewed water into the basement, and the only thing to do was shut my house down for a month or two.

DEX WAS HAPPY to let me crash on his couch. He had a place in the Cass Corridor down near Masonic, a shitty place in a fifteen-story building, but it had heat, and he was obsessive about keeping it clean and relatively roachless. It always amazed me that he managed to hold onto his double bass despite the obvious logic of pawning it. He kept it leaned against the wall, a shotgun right alongside it with a streak of rust down its barrel.

SINCE WE WERE living together all through December, we practiced every day. We did the standards: "Greensleeves," "Summer Time," even "My Favorite Things." Always ending with his song, Dexter's Song, playing it over and over, trying to get it right. I hit that sax so hard I almost cried. I mean I dumped everything in it. Everything. That Selmer made it easy, so damn perfect were the notes flying from its bell. Meanwhile Dex thumped away on the bass, keeping time, walking up and down its long neck. It was an exhausting effort, but amazing. Every time we played, I felt my soul rising through my skin and filling the room. I don't know if he felt that way too, but there was something very good and pure about his song. It was weird, though, because the more we practiced it, the less we seemed to be able to end it. I knew Dex was searching for a finish to it, for some way to rein us back in, but so far it wasn't exactly happening. I was just blowing my brains out, blowing and blowing, and then ending abruptly, completely exhausted, covered with sweat, ache in my throat. My God, we kept working on it. It was getting better, but I was getting worse, and I needed a hit, something good, something to settle me down, to smooth out the barbs of the world. The more alive I felt, the more likely it seemed that I would die.

THE DAY AFTER Christmas, Sabrina's parents left again, this time to Florida, and she invited me up to stay at her place. So I left Dexter's and practiced the Selmer, solo, in the warm light of her living room. Only I didn't have my bike, so I found the keys to her parents' BMW. I found other things too, things I could trade or pawn, little things no one would miss. I know it was shitty, but staying doped was hard. I rationed myself, stretching my stash as best I could, but still I'd run out and be stuck. I knew this whole arrangement wasn't going to work for long.

She was no idiot. She knew I had a problem. I tried to quit, but every night I sweated through her sheets all down to the mattress, and just sat there shaking. Sabrina was decent about it. I don't know why because it was not cool. I was sick as fuck. I was dying here. I should die here. I should shoot my brains out. I didn't want to talk about what I really needed, but I had too.

I needed a ride, like now, please? Two in the morning, it didn't matter. All I really needed was a ride to Bullet's place. Everything would be OK.

I can't believe I'm doing this, she said. But she did.

Tried and true, Bullet was up, waiting for me, and I snorted just enough to get my blood pumping right, and get me home so I could make up a needle. It was that good-easy *Horse Head* that was making everything right again.

Instead of taking me back to the burbs, she dropped me back at Dexter's.

You're a fucking train wreck, she said. Get out of my car. She was crying when I closed the door of her car and walked into the tenement. I felt alright. I was back in the zone, an OK place for now. I didn't hear from her for a long week after. Part of me really missed her, but mostly I kept myself medicated. I was OK.

I WASN'T LYING when I said I had never heard of the Selmer, Mark VI. It was Dexter who found out that this was the same horn on which Coltrane blew out his bad-ass brains. He was a dope head too. I wonder how he kicked it. I know he did. I was stuck for the time being. In a way though, I felt a real connection with him. It seemed like this horn might just change my life, so beautiful were the notes it shaped. It might just save me. I think as I was learning how to play through it, it was learning how to play through me. If that makes sense. Maybe Sabrina didn't know about its value either, or maybe she didn't care. Money didn't mean as much to her. In any case, I was keeping it safe, and I promised not to pawn or trade it. No matter what.

REALLY, I DIDN'T know anything much about Lars, her ex-husband, until he was dead. Of course I listened to Sabrina complain that he wasted his talents playing Kenny G tunes. I couldn't tell you what that means, only I guess that it was smooth, so smooth it might not even be jazz, just something to stroke your dick to, and not a hard dick either. If Lars was dull, that was OK by me. She blamed it on his job. Even though he made a shit ton, all that boring corporate work made his blood go gray. I asked her once how much she thought he would take for the horn.

Do you think he would take fifteen hundred?

She just laughed.

Screw him, she said.

I wondered how many I-beams I'd need to harvest for that kind of dough. I couldn't think clear enough to do the math, but I had a sense of the size building that would collapse for the cost of the horn. Only if Sabrina would talk to him, maybe we could set up a payment plan.

I'LL NEVER UNDERSTAND exactly why Sabrina told Lars where I was staying. It must have been out of some exasperation with me. I swear I didn't have anything to do with anything that went down that day. It was just that her ex is so damn white, so damn Kenny G. And he came sauntering into the tenement full of prostitutes and heroin addicts and freaky fucking crackheads. Who knows what he left on his car seat. I wasn't there to witness his windows being broken out. All I know is that there was no reason to stomp up the stairs and pound on our door and demand that I open it, yelling my name, and saying the police were on their way. I guess he didn't know anything about anything. Dexter and I had been doping all day. I told him not to answer and I took the horn and climbed through the window and up the fire escape to the empty flat above.

Somehow Dexter slipped a cog. Maybe all the yelling flipped some sort of switch in him. I don't know. But I'm sure he wasn't thinking when he unlatched the door and leveled the barrel of his shotgun at Lars. I was upstairs, warming up the Selmer, holding the reed in my mouth and blowing air through its shining body, when a blast shuddered through the building.

EVERYTHING THAT FOLLOWED was a disaster. The violence of Lars's death was sudden and terrible. Even though I didn't know him, it left something black and sad aching in my chest. It sucked at me, hissed, as if my lungs had sprung leaks. I couldn't play. It was hard to think of anything else. For all of February and part of March, it seemed like I was going to lose the sax, but through some wrangling Sabrina managed, I was able to keep it.

Then apparently the *Detroit White* that Bullet sold me in place of *Horse Head* was cut with some bad shit, fentanyl or something. I don't blame him, but also I do. He should have told me more. I know I was eager to try it, and I made up my needle a little on the heavy side. The shit hit me like a bulldozer and mashed me to the floor. I couldn't do anything but lie there, spreading out, and so what if Sabrina was screaming, her bird voice filling the room. I let her slap me so many times in the same spot and didn't even flinch. I was up, standing over my body, which was black and flat as shadow, watching those fuckers shoot my heart full of some shit. I wanted them to stop. They were killing my buzz. Making me sick. A man with hooks for hands dug into my ribs. Then my feet were dragging down the stairs, thumping heavily on the carpet. I could hear them talking about me. I was the star out there in the night, flicking with light. I could wear this oxygen mask forever. The siren was playing its own song, not a very good one. I guess their drugs were working, because I was thinking of Lars and how stupid he was. Feeling the motion of the vehicle as we turned the corner. The roar of the engine.

I WOKE IN a hospital room. People said I was lucky to be alive. I didn't feel lucky. No one was happy, but at least here I didn't have to lie about anything. My situation was obvious. I was a sorry piece of shit.

I wanted to quit the dope. I really did. The truth I told Sabrina was this: Coltrane kicked the dope. I think I can too. Fact is, I was born in a hospital in Detroit, at almost the moment that Coltrane died. I don't know if that makes me special or what, but I think it might. July 17, 1967, and one week later, the city exploded with riots and looting and burning, and stupid cops and National Guard killing people. Maybe while smoke drifted between buildings and Coltrane was becoming part of the universe, maybe he became part of me too. All I know is this horn, this Selmer, is something real special. It is delivering me to a new plane of thought. For that I am thankful. And yes, I promise to kick the dope. Coltrane did. I can too.

IT WAS APRIL and Dexter was fucked. He was caught up in the legal system, going to prison, probably forever. He had a decent lawyer, and even a pretty good case, but the costs were out of hand. Meanwhile I was clean still. It's not like I didn't think about it, but I kept my head down and worked through the day, unmedicated.

I guess it was around the end of the month when Sabrina called in a favor and was somehow able to get me on the schedule at this club called Trinosophes. We set it up as a benefit to help Dexter with his legal costs. The owners agreed to pay us door, which came to about $400. It wasn't a lot, but it meant something. It meant a lot. The room filled with Dex's old friends, some from as far back as high school. I guess word about his trouble spread quickly, and the newspaper picked it up too.

I was surprised to see Bullet in the audience. He was sitting with some big shot or whoever from New York. Only Sabrina would never forgive me if I talked to him. So I kept my distance. I just waited until the room filled, then got on stage. It was just me. Solo on Selmer. I only had one song to play, but it was a doozie. I stretched it for almost thirty minutes. It was Dexter's Song. I started slow and sweet, then rose way up there, right into the truss work, hovering above the crowd and blowing like crazy, moving through major thirds, perfect fourths. Man, I was soaring, over-blowing, working in circular motion, breathing but not stopping for breath, hitting those notes so hard and holding them until they softened into sweet moans. I pushed on, working my way through the harmonics, determined not to let it get away from me. I found my way right into the very core of the song and let the melody roll from my lungs, through the reed and brass body of that horn. I shut my eyes and arched back, and blew like crazy, calling for Coltrane, that he might rise and breathe through me, and float from this horn, to ascend naked and new and carry me to my fucking grave. I don't know if

I ever played so well. There was just so much to say. All I know is that every note I formed, whether squonk or scream or tender low hum, each felt like it had been there for a reason. When I was done, I found I could stand no longer. I released the Selmer from my lips and sat on the edge of the stage, completely exhausted, and listened only to the strange good sound of the clapping audience.

IT WAS ALMOST impossible to quit the dope, but really I tried. It's just the hardest thing to not take a breath when you need to breathe. Still, I took my points and spoon and rubber tubing, and tossed it all in the dumpster, and watched as the city truck hoisted it up and swallowed its contents. All was not lost, even with Dexter stuck in jail, and the difficult misery of Lars's death, knowing that Sabrina was still grieving him. Maybe that was part of the reason she decided to move in with me. She had quit drinking and was making a project of fixing my life. I didn't complain. I liked having her around, and truly things were changing because of her. The house looked different, that's for sure. She started by pulling the vines that had grown through the walls. She called for a tow truck to drag away the rotted Winnebago that sat for years overgrown with ghetto palm. Then, without asking, she made an order with the electric company to install a new service drop because the generator was constantly ruining the air with its stink.

Except for coons and pheasants, we were mostly alone on this block, and at night we loved hard and frequently. We both knew that something good was happening here.

Every day after we got the dishes cleaned up, I took the Selmer and walked into the field to the pond beyond my property line, where the land had sunk due to some infrastructure failure, and stood in the fading sunlight, and played a slower, sweeter version of Dexter's song. The notes shimmered in the dusk and rose into the sky with upward energy, lifting toward the small handful of stars that shined over the city. I played it like a prayer. I listened for some answer, but it was hard to hear past the quick pulse of the peepers. Each day the grass was a little less brown, and the broken bottles that strewed the neighboring lots were beginning to disappear too. Summer was coming and bringing with it the idea that warm sun and rain might just fix everything. It was crawling north from Ohio, and soon it would turn the whole place green. I guess I was calling for that too. I was playing Dexter's song, and would keep playing it until my lungs ran out of air, and I know every time I did, it was a little better too. I'm not sure when I would be done, or if it would ever be perfect, but I would keep playing it until somehow I got it right.

Part Plant, Part Animal, Part Insect

The thing about a Stupor is that if you're in one, you stop wanting or even needing to want, because how do you want if you can't think? At least that's how Tim put it. Even though I have tried, I have never stopped wanting. I always wanted the wanting to stop, but how could I when, for example, I was on the couch next to Jackie, and she was studying her data sheets while Tim was in the other room praying to the Great Good? I could never ignore Jackie, and if she noticed me gazing, she might rake her dark hair from her lips, lick her finger a little too intentionally, then turn a page. Or maybe she would lean her shoulder to mine as if to whisper, but instead kiss the inside of my ear, allowing her tongue to stroll around my auricle, into my external acoustic meatus. What a bizarre feeling. So strange! She would do that, and end it just as abruptly. Her eyes stayed focused and narrow as she turned back to her paperwork. She was a sweet lusty swamp; every part of her was asking to be needed. No matter how much beer I drank, every part of me needed her too, but she was Tim's. It was a painful situation.

EACH OF US held a biochemistry degree. We first met at work. They hired us right out of college. Jackie from Oxford, Tim from Harvard, and me from Wayne State University in Detroit. Preferred Poultry was the company. The difficult truth is that within two years of landing the job, Tim developed a procedure to grow chickens from seeds, which bypassed the whole egg and hatching issue. It seemed impossible, but it worked. Despite the weirdness of the process, the meat tasted better than a regular hatched bird. But it was a mistake ever working there. We were tinkering with nature, and after a while, it messed with us bad, especially Tim.

Shortly after Tim's eureka moment, his grandmother was killed. It was a mostly sunny afternoon, but from one single dark cloud, a bolt of lightning shot to the earth, striking her and her metal shopping cart. She just was coming back from the corner grocery, and she was incinerated. Her cart melted into a shining puddle. Subsequently, he inherited her house, which stood in a mostly empty Detroit neighborhood. That's where we all lived, his grandma's old place. It was a little musty but pretty nice, with her frilly curtains and antique furniture. The streets surrounding it were broken up, some completely overgrown, and pheasants and deer and coons wandered the fields around us. One road, two blocks away, had permanently flooded, and was now full of cattails and frogs and insects of all kinds. It became the Stupor House. That's what we called it.

THE IDEA THAT we should make our own instruments came to Tim in a prayer. One night, very late, we had just turned out the lights and lay in the dark, wrapped in blankets, buzzing on wine and whiskey. Tim was going on about the Great Good, and Jackie—I don't know. She rolled against me, right over my arm, and in the darkness, I pressed my fingers to her shoulders and held her. She took my other hand and placed it on her chest. Tim talked on. He was explaining how music might be interpreted as a series of codes, and how the right code might set things straight again because now they were all out of whack. I was just barely digesting his idea when Jackie opened her robe and pushed down the elastic of my underwear. She pulled me closer and closer and a charge crackled in my skin. I was only in her for one amazing minute, but that was enough. I pressed my mouth hard against hers to avoid hollering. All my muscles seized and a quick spark leapt from me into the deepest part of her. When it was over, we lay there in darkness, breathing fast, stupid, glowing with guilt. She laid her head against my shoulder, made soft snoring sounds, while Tim kept talking and figuring, making plans with himself.

I GOT THE feeling that sex for Jackie was just a necessary annoyance, like flossing or something. She just didn't seem to feel it like I did. That morning following our romp was incredibly difficult. We all sat together in the kitchen and ate breakfast. I was giddy and zinging with shame. I had barely slept. Jackie took the seat between me and Tim, her robe cinched together at her waist but loose around her chest. I turned my head and sat there, staring at the egg scramble she had whipped up, then accidently dumped salt in my coffee. Tim grabbed my hand, laughing, and told me to relax. What's up brother? he asked. What could I say? My brain had been reduced to a thousand little bubbles, each a soapy heart with Jackie's name smeared across it. I couldn't look up without slipping into the tender gorge between her breasts. My brain was simply gone. It had been sucked from my mouth and spat on the floor. We ate in silence, and when we were done, Tim announced that he had extracted some powerful ideas through his conversations with the Great Good. He had been given information about how we might build instruments. He would start working on them right after he was finished with his coffee. And he did.

FOR JACKIE, HE fabricated two fibrous wing-like structures, which, when rubbed together, created an unearthly rhythmic hum. Then he strapped the contraption to her thighs and positioned contact microphones where the wings met her skin. She played by rubbing them together. When she really got it going, she could take the house down. I mean the intonation was so powerful it could shake mortar from brick. As if that wasn't enough, it seemed to give her tremendous sexual power over the audience. Tim spent his weeks studying the exact mechanism that insects use to chirp and attract a mate. He modified it to make a human version of the call, discovering that imbedded within a particular timbre and tonality were ancient messages that could only be decoded by chemical receptors in a listener's testicles. It was the sound of love and desire. It was irresistible and made Jackie more magnificent than ever. On stage, she became the pure essence of sexual energy.

For himself, Tim installed electrodes between varying points on his body, and connected them with little red wires to a transmitter he strapped to his back. He used his actual physical impulses to trigger a synthesizer mechanism, which converted the varying pulses to a series of corresponding notes. It required a lot of weird jerking movements and caused him to sweat profusely. I know it was a difficult intellectual effort to listen and respond to what Jackie and I were doing, and in the process build a melody simply through movement. That's what he did. It blew my mind.

For me, he developed what we called the Stuporstick. It's made from a six-foot limb of a sugar maple. Tim shaved its bark, notched it with a knife, glued and screwed guitar pickups under a long, fretless column of twenty wire-wound strings, all of varying length and thickness. Before I stepped on stage, I wrapped myself in fronds mostly from the fern, which grew wild in the shady lots around the Stupor House. The outfit was somewhat cumbersome. Still, I felt comfortable in it since I was more or less camouflaged, and if something happened and I could not control my physical responses in relation to Jackie, at least for the most part, any sort of unintended sexual exhibition would be hidden by the foliage.

TOGETHER, WE WERE part plant, part animal, and part insect. We were Stupor. We were the tactile sound experience of desire. We were creating wants, but doing our best to ignore our own wants—at least while we were playing. We were mining songs from the deepest part of the universe. But also our music was like everything you have already heard, only never noticed. We were deconstructing sound and rebuilding it through our bodies.

In a way, our music was a necessary apology to the world for what we accomplished at work. Think of it. There was a huge pole barn in the middle of the field where houses had once stood. Large as an airplane hangar, it stood very prominent under the sky, surrounded by ghetto palms. You could not deny its existence. The walls stood as truth. You could walk up and touch them. They were hot from the baking sun. Most people assumed that nothing bad was going on in there, because it was dressed up to look a certain way, but what we were doing was growing birds from seeds. We were damning ourselves, tinkering with the mechanism of creation. We shouldn't have done that. So as a means of reconciliation, we played music.

Henceforth, our lab discussions became a framework for songs. But the real music didn't happen until Tim rigged himself with electrodes and prayed particular prayers. Not only did he feed his wires to the synthesizer, he also was connected to an electrocardiograph machine that we bought off Craigslist. It printed a graphic version of each song, which became our sheet music—a scroll of chaotic but beautiful scribble. I can't tell you how many times Jackie and I watched from the other room as Tim, in reverie and prayer, shook and squirmed with sound. It was fascinating and gruesome too. We'd sit there on the carpet, our backs against the couch, just watching him flip around. Finally, when he was done, she would get up and kiss him right in front of me. I hated that. I knew she loved him, but please! Have some sympathy.

IN THOSE DAYS, I was living for the ten minutes that Jackie gave me every morning when she pulled back my sheets and slid her body against mine. It wasn't much, but I accepted it and tried to feel lucky for the little I had. I just wanted to be happy. I know Jackie did too. Only it was really hard, since I was no more than this little compartment of her day. I don't know how she could just turn on and off like that. I thought of her all the time—I still do—though she barely had but a few sweet, sweaty minutes for me.

IT WAS TIM'S old friend Gilbert that put our first show together. The venue was the VFW post 323. I remember there was something wrong with the wiring in that building. The energy just barely worked, and when we cranked our amps, the sound was loud and crisp, but the lights in the rest of the place drained down to zero. At one point I looked out the window and saw the moon. It was weird because the louder we played, the more its light seemed to dim. We kept the show going for five amazing hours. Later we made a bonfire in the parking lot, and the flames rose into the sky with a tremendous heat. Tim, still grease-coated, wrapped his arms around Jackie, and she put her hand on me, resting it on the bracken fronds that twisted from my shoulders, and I reached around her and ran my hand over her smooth, solid hips, and there we stood, the three of us, not saying anything, just pressed together under the stars. It would have been a good photo. The flames snapped and flicked light all over us.

I feel like a veteran, Tim said. Only the war we are fighting is on the cellular scale.

I didn't care what he said. I couldn't quite intellectualize the experience. It was such a good show, so emotional, completely cathartic. Tim's brain had jumped alive. Ideas were flying from him, popping and spitting like little bits of burnt filament.

PART OF TIM'S brilliance bordered on an eccentricity that I didn't completely understand. For example, he was very serious about greasing his clothes. He used chicken fat. Not only because we had access to an abundance of it, but apparently it reflected cosmic rays, which otherwise seeped into his skin and messed with his ability to think clearly. Everything got better when coated with grease. It became a necessary component of Stupor shows. Jackie made it happen. She had clearance to that particular lab where the reconstituted chicken fat was stored, so she would slice off big chunks of the slimy yellow goop, wrap it in paper, and stick it in her bag. Then an hour or so before we played, Tim softened the stuff in his hands until it was spreadable. With a spatula, he smeared his coveralls. It gave our performances a strange scent, as if some delicious dinner was cooking. Of course, when he played, his body would heat up until gradually the grease melted and ran all over the floor, creating a very slippery situation, which was part of how we were able to move so fluidly without even lifting our feet, and also part of why at some point during every show, we all flipped on our backs and played to the sky.

IN THE SPRING of 2012, Tim's old friend Gilbert turned up again. He was pounding on the door of the Stupor House, a black garbage bag full of clothes slung over his shoulder, his face dotted with scabs, his skin far too wrinkled for someone who was no doubt five years younger than me. Along with Gilbert came a heap of trouble. He carried it deep within his cells, but then dumped it quickly all over our living room. Within a day, his clothes were strewn everywhere, and the couch was torn apart, so it was hard to find a place to sit. It seemed that he had the potential to ruin everything he touched. Certainly, he took my faith in Jackie and cracked it like an egg and swallowed it, then sat there grinning.

THERE WERE PROBLEMS, that's for sure, and Gilbert was the source. The worst was when I found him and Jackie out in the parking lot behind a VFW hall we had just played. They were in the front seat of a car, and her shirt was pushed apart, and he had a handful of her skin gripped in his palm; and her poor nipple bulged forth, squeezed to an unnatural shape, while he mauled her with kisses. We made eye contact, she and I.

Her lips formed the words Go away.

She might just as well have taken an auger to me, and drilled a hole through my chest, and packed it tight with her dirty underwear and wet toilet paper. It wasn't fair. From that point on, I dedicated myself to pointing out his flaws. They were obvious. It's gross having scabs on your face. Only thing was, Tim really gelled with him. Another day, I caught him and Jackie snorting meth or coke or whatever. I was so pissed at her. I know that stuff can explode your heart, but Gilbert just laughed.

IT WAS NO real surprise, at least to me, when his just rewards came as a drug-related heart attack. The funeral was a solid hundred miles from Detroit, out on a country road, near his parents' house. I was surprised that Tim volunteered us to play his wake. We had to bring a generator because the power was insufficient, and there he was, in a gaudy silver casket in the middle of a double wide trailer-home that looked like it had been decorated by Liberace himself. We set up around the body and proceeded to play one of the most beautiful shows ever. The entire room whirled and soared with sound. At one point, Tim laid a microphone on Gilbert's chest. He had this idea that some remaining impulse in the body might surface even though his lips were obviously glued shut. I guess the show gave me a chance to forgive him. I tried, but I couldn't. I just kept thinking of all the times he pawed Jackie.

WITHOUT GILBERT, THE future held more serious possibilities. We all had ambitions, both scientific and musical. One day Jackie, in some brainy experiment, developed a chicken that was twice the size of a normal bird, and had multiple breasts and legs. It was a terrifying Franken-chicken. Of course the head of the company was thrilled and called her personally into his office to celebrate with a bottle of champagne. She came back to the lab giddy and flushed. Apparently, during the meeting, he told her that she would need to turn over her notes to the patent team. Within a half hour, I found Tim in the restroom, tearing pages from her lab book, stuffing the paper in his mouth and chewing it up. He ripped out a handful and told me to eat. We sat there draining our coffee cups and cramming tedious descriptions of Jackie's experiments into our mouths. It was difficult, but I knew it had to be done. There were cameras in the building. It wasn't long before the security thugs grabbed us, squeezed the blood from our arms, and shoved us into the parking lot. Getting fired from that job was devastating, but also one of the best things that ever happened. Shortly after we got canned, Jackie quit too.

OUR PERIOD OF unemployment was artistically fertile, but fraught with trouble. We made an album, our only album, and pressed it to vinyl. After listening to it, Tim seriously slipped a cog. He tore through the Stupor House, smashing his fist into the walls. Then one by one, he raised the boxes of our record over his head and smashed them on the floor. Something had gone wrong in him. When he was done, he sat in the middle of the wreckage, a stunned look on his face. I couldn't understand. He kept saying that this physical representation of the music was antithetical to our mission in the world.

It has to remain spiritual if we are going to be effective, he said.

All I can say is that I had a deep intellectual respect for him, so I helped carry the boxes into the empty lot across the street, the one grown thick with weed trees and the high swaying grass. Late that night, he emptied a bottle of lighter fluid over the heap and tossed in a match. The blaze was a bright pillar climbing into the sky. It made an awful smell. Incidentally, the album was called *Gallus Gallus*, which is the scientific name for chicken. It was an amazing record. I deeply regret not keeping more than one copy.

SOON AFTER THE release and ruin of our record, things got worse. Terribly worse. Our last show took place on a stage that Tim built by laying squares of plywood over the weeds next to the Stupor House. It was muggy, and there was a hot, unsettling breeze. Maybe fifty diehard fans showed up. As the evening wore on, the weather turned, and soon, just into our third hour, the sky sucked to black and began flashing with lightning, but Tim would not quit. Truly, his playing was brilliant. Jackie too, she moaned and buzzed. As she sawed her thighs together, I felt my hold on reality slipping. She had seeped into my blood and beat against my veins. I stiffened and bent, but instead of giving into her and ripping away her clothes, I forced all my energy into my instrument, and smacked the end of my Stuporstick hard on the plywood. Sound crashed from us in wild musical swirls. The lightning kept getting closer and I knew we were going to have to quit soon, but Tim was experiencing an ecstatic freak-out, dripping with sweat and chicken grease. I could taste the rain in the air. We were going to get soaked. Still, our fans were sticking with us. Tim kept on, his eyes rolling back in his head, but then suddenly, it was too late. With a blinding crash, a huge splintering bolt of lightning blew the back off the Stupor House. You can't plan for an explosion like that. It shook the earth. It split the very air, ripping its molecules to little filmy bits of smoke. It was deafening. I don't know how we could have known, but the massive masonry chimney had flipped over and skid from the eaves, tearing away the gutter. I didn't have time to look or push Tim out of the way. I only felt the terrible dull thud. It flattened him. It pushed him right through the plywood and into the ground. There was no hope. The rain started in a rush, roaring and pounding with such a fury that I could barely see. I knew I needed to get that chimney off Tim, but it was so heavy. It was impossible. It took five of us to get an angle on it and roll it away. By that time, it was too late. He was gone. There was absolutely no way to bring him back. I kept waiting for someone to rescue us, to reverse time and end this whole bad dream. I just couldn't stop shivering. The rain made a blur of it. It turned the soil to mud. Jackie kneeled in it, holding Tim's one good hand.

NOT LONG AFTER Tim's death, our boss at the chicken factory sent a letter describing how grateful he was to have had Tim as a former member of the research team. Apparently his work on the Chicken Seed had been the beginning of huge profits. He included a check in condolence that more than paid for the funeral, and along with it was a request that we consider playing a memorial show at Preferred Poultry. It was disgusting even considering it. I mean this building that housed all those awful smells, with snowy feathers constantly flying through the air, surrounded by thousands of gallus gallus. But we did do a small memorial for Tim on his uncle's farm, just north of the city, up Van Dyke and into the thumb. We played in a barn for a small group of friends. The building rippled with sound. The acoustics were surprisingly good. It was inspiring. Only I kept turning to look at Tim for my cues, but there was only Jackie, rubbing her thighs together, a rumbling hum coming from her. She was weeping but smiling, her face a stream of shining tears. We kept on, and gradually, after several hours of playing, we put down our instruments, and that's when I realized that the barn had filled with dozens of white birds. They sat very still, lining the beams. They were mesmerized. It was a beautiful moment.

WITHOUT TIM, NOTHING made much sense. Still, I felt lucky and thankful that Jackie was alive. One night at the bar, I asked her to leave this city with me. I told her I had fishing gear, rod and reel and tons of lures, and also I had a couple acres in the Upper Peninsula. She sat there looking into her glass and nodded, but then after a moment shook her head no. Her eyes were dry and distant. She was opaque to me. Maybe we had run our course. We grew and grew and grew and then simply got crushed. Part of me was starving for something new. Part of me was still just starving for her. The next day, I packed my stuff and drove straight up the middle of the state. It took me only a week to find a job. I was lucky. I got hired as a short-order cook at a place on 41, Jerry's Hometown Diner, just outside of Marquette. Mostly, I grilled sandwiches and dunked French fries into hot oil and kept to myself, but at the end of my shift, I'd make a burger and sit at the counter with a bowl of whatever soup was left over. Sometimes Jerry would break out a bottle, and we'd fire back a couple shots before I headed out into the night. He knew I was looking for a house and told me he was glad I planned to stick around. All I knew was that I needed to find a place soon. Fall was coming quick, and by the end of October snow would fly like a motherfucker. I wanted to pick up something small, maybe a cabin, hopefully not far from a stream, where I could fish for trout. I wanted a place where I could raise chickens the old-fashioned way, maybe just for their eggs, and enough land to grow tomatoes and beans too, and to hopefully keep my fridge full of beer. Once I get set up, I'm going to call Jackie. She doesn't know it, but I think we can be happy again. I am planning it all. I just never stopped thinking about her. Even here at the diner with my back to the fogged windows, I'm warming a seat, just for her.

New Phase

After I hear the mailman flipping the lid on our box, I dunk my brush in the turpentine and bound down from my studio, grabbing a bag of potato chips as I pass through the kitchen. Here it is. Oh shit. The envelope has a cloth weave. The name of the foundation is inked in the corner. I hold my breath and rip into it, but I pretty much already know. Though my name is printed on the first line, it's obviously a form letter. It says it all real nice too, but what it comes down to is my work is not good enough. Once again, I didn't make the cut. Fuckers!

Well, now I am stuck. I can't paint or anything. I sit on the concrete porch sweating and feeling heavy.

The old man who lives next door pulls up in his new Bronco. Hey Andrew, how's it going in there, he asks.

OK, I say. Just plugging away.

He looks skeptical. I pick up my phone and pretend I'm on a call until he leaves.

I know the neighbors were surprised when Patti and I moved in, because how can anyone live in a junk house like this, especially with such a big hole gaping in the roof. It's true the place isn't exactly habitable, but we make do. I think of it like camping. We're camping in this house.

I sit on the porch smoking cigarettes until finally Patti roars down the street in her Chevy van. I am extra hungry today, and so is she. We have flour and sugar, so I mix us some pancakes and fry up a pound of bacon. She is not thrilled about me skipping out on my diet, but there are a lot of things I am not thrilled about too. For one, I worked my ass off on the grant application, only to receive that dumb letter in the mail. For another, she is too lazy to change out of her work duds and wears them at the table. Tonight, she smells something like a hamster cage. Not wanting to start anything, I focus on my plate, soaking the pancakes in syrup. We pass the canister of whipped cream between us and take turns spurting out heaps of the fluffy stuff.

I'm starving again. I try my best not to make sounds when I eat, but here and there my breathing turns to little snorts. I look up at her, hoping she didn't hear. But she is staring, shaking her head. Patti, I say, I'm famished.

You're doing it again.

I'm sorry. But pancakes are delicious. The bacon is like heaven. I shovel it in. I wait for her to say something more. I know what she's thinking. I am still the pig I was when she met me. I can't help it. I love to eat, and so does she. She is just blessed with a fierce metabolism. It keeps her skinny and beautiful and impossible.

After dinner, I leave the sticky plates and the batter bowl in the sink. I vow to clean up later and head back to my studio, where I begin stretching a new canvas. After Patti is showered and clean, she walks through the room with a towel on her head, then sits her skinny butt before me on a metal stool. She has mixed some sort of drink and sets it on my worktable and proceeds to comb her hair.

Did you hear that Fernando won one of those grants? she says.

Fernando? You're kidding. My God, I really toiled over that application. It took forever. I can't believe he got it.

He got it for his bird uniforms. It was all over Facebook.

Oh, now I hate Fernando even more.

He's not so hateable.

He makes bird costumes! How is that art? It's depressing.

Yeah, well they're really good bird costumes.

They're still just fucking bird costumes! It doesn't matter if they're good. They're stupid. They're not art. They suck.

Maybe you need to think a little more about losing some weight and less about hating Fernando.

I wish you wouldn't turn it all back on me. I feel crappy enough.

I'm just sick of you hating on Fernando.

I don't hate all your exes. Just Fernando. Why are you defending him?

I'm not. I'm just saying.

She looks around the room and her eyes land on the painting that I started last week. It's only one layer of work. Very sloppy. Her gaze drifts upward to the rafters, then to the large hole in the roof. When are you going to fix that?

What's the use? I say. But we do have an arrangement with our landlord. In exchange for a discount on our rent, I am supposed to fix the house up a little every month. So far I'm not doing much to improve it. Certainly, though, this is not just a little project.

Except for the kitchen ceiling, most of the plaster is smashed away, exposing long, rough-hewn 2x4s. It's true there is a hole in the roof for the birds to fly through. A big hole. It's about the size of a large appliance. For the life of me, I can't imagine what caused it. The sparrows and the chimney sweeps like it. They sit on the collar ties, singing to each other. Their little white splatters need to be washed away daily, but as long as they don't poop on my paintings, I don't mind.

Actually, I like having it open. At night, after the birds leave, you can stand under it and look out at the sky, up past the long boughs of the basswood tree. Here and there a star shows through; maybe the moon makes a pass, too, and shines its pale light on us.

It's not very late, but Patti is tired. From what she tells me, working at the zoo is demanding, so I understand when she runs out of steam before I do. She pulls the plastic covering from the bed and spreads out on the sheets. Maybe her dinner isn't sitting right, or maybe it's the drinks, or just the tension regarding Fernando, but something is wrong. After another cigarette, I remove my clothes and lie down too. We listen to the city. A car blasts down our street. It stops and honks. Loud music rattles from it. We lie side by side, barely touching. It's true that I've put on a little more weight since we moved in, and I know that's a problem, but that doesn't mean we can't have sex. My plumbing is still highly functional. So I don't know what it is that has us at odds. Just as we are almost asleep, a car thumps past with the flatulent rhythm of a flat tire. We hear this every night at least once.

THE FOLLOWING AFTERNOON, I am sitting on the porch, picking at the green scum of moss that grows on the decking. I'm just finishing a smoke break when a tow truck rumbles down our street and comes to a stop in front of our house. I'm surprised when Patti climbs out.

Where's the van? I say.

Oh, it's been a helluva day, she says with a weird smile. The van is busted.

Oh no.

All it does it bust. It drives good for a month and then loses a bearing, breaks a spring, squirts fluid into the air, drips, oozes, sits there looking ornery, tired of its own van-ness. This vehicle is out to get us.

What happened?

The wheel fell off.

No!

I was only just barely pulling out of the parking lot. It made this terrible clunk. I thought I'd hit some giant Detroit pothole. Then I saw a wheel rolling down the street, and I'm thinking, Oh my God, how bizarre! Someone lost a wheel. I'm thinking maybe it hit me or something, but then I realized it was my wheel. It shot down the service drive and disappeared onto the entrance ramp of the highway. What could I do but throw up my hands?

Then out of the blue, Fernando shows up, and he's totally stoned and dressed as a big white owl. I can't stop laughing. I mean, I'm almost hysterical because I've completely given up hope. Fernando is sort of bobbing around saying weird things about the blueness of the sky. Has it never been so blue? I have no idea what he's talking about. Everyone is staring and slowing down to get a look at him. He digs around in his feathery butt and extracts a motor club card.

I still hate him, I say.

You need to get over that. I invited him for dinner. He's coming after his lecture, OK? He said he'd bring a pizza or something.

Oh God, you're not serious.

I am. I'm serious.

Why she'd invite anyone here is beyond me. I guess that's when I realize that I could sure benefit from a drink right now. This is a bad day to be on a diet. I head straight to the fridge and open one of her big bottles of Colt 45.

Andrew, she says, what are you doing?

I'm drinking malt liquor. Maybe you should too.

I look up at the kitchen ceiling, which is still spotted with drips of orange grease, not our fault. It really bothers me that I haven't even thought of how to clean it. I should have knocked it out long ago.

Lots of calories in there. Probably not the best idea for you to drink all that.

Probably not. Do you want some?

Of course.

I hand her the large bottle and she upends it, and bubbles rise to foam in the clear glass. After we kill the beer, the mechanic shop calls. They're quick at least. She covers the mouthpiece.

They want $450 to fix the front end. What do I tell them?

I don't know. Tell them we're broke. Ask about a payment plan.

OK, she says to the phone, ignoring me. Go ahead and fix it.

I know it's going to take some figuring to come up with the cash. If only I could sell a painting. Something like that would be so helpful. It would be the boost I need to feel like it's all worth it and I'm not just wasting my life on something that no one cares about.

There's a slight breeze coming in through the open windows. It rises through the house and probably out the hole in the roof.

What is that smell? Is that you? I ask.

I think it is.

Giraffe poop?

She sniffs at her arms. That's not giraffe. I think it's from the ape house. I had to work there most of the day. And that big bastard Charlie was throwing feces again. I better clean up before Fernando gets here.

While she's showering, I get out the mop, committing myself to a minor step forward. I work on the kitchen ceiling. Maybe it's cooking oil that covers everything, or maybe someone came in with a shook-up can of Coke and sprayed the place. The sticky stuff clings to the plastic bobbles of the 70s chandelier. It gathers in amber droplets. I discover that a sponge mop works pretty well on it. I can safely say that I have never lived anywhere where I had to mop the ceiling.

Water is still dripping from the plaster when Patti comes walking through the room naked, combing her wet hair. Already the pads of her feet are dark with dirt. Really this is no place to walk with bare feet, not without an update on your tetanus shot. I'm troubled by it. I mean, if you're going to go through the effort of washing, then don't go walking around the filthy house in bare feet. They are instantly dirty again. This is why our bedsheets need to be washed so much. Flip-flops are such an easy solution, but she simply doesn't care.

Maybe we can sell the noodle maker your aunt gave you, she says. She shoos the cat off the couch, pulls back the dusty plastic tarp, and sits down, and now is probably getting lint and little hairs stuck to her legs, her back, her rump. Makes me crazy.

How are we going to make noodles without my noodle machine?

We're not. We'll just buy them like normal people. They're cheap.

The doorbell is ringing.

Fernando, is that you? She calls from the couch.

It's me.

I huff into the room and wait for Patti to unfold the afghan and cover herself. She does, but the weave is pretty loose and allows her nipples to pop through. What the hell does it matter?

Fernando stands in the doorway wearing his elaborate snowy owl costume, smelling strongly of weed, looking completely ridiculous. He removes his feathery helmet. Hello, my friends, he says. His eyes are narrow and red, but smiling all the same. What a day, huh? He is holding two pizza boxes and six-pack under his wing. I brought you all some goodies. Oh my God, I love your house. It's so perfect.

Perfect for birds, I say.

I love it! He tilts back to take in all the bare studs, the exposed ceiling joists, and the neat lines of the knob and tube wiring. Oh, I do love it.

I look down the street and see it's all parked up. Did you have trouble finding a spot?

Huh?

A parking spot.

I flew, man. I'm good. I strapped the pizza on my back. Flapped my wings. No problem.

You flew?

Yeah, it's not too windy or anything. Pretty good day for flying.

You're going to get your nice white feathers all dirty in here, Patti says.

Ah, my feathers are self-cleaning. He waddles into the house and I pull the plastic from the easy chair. He sets the pizza down on the floor.

Hey Patti, where did your clothes go?

It's my house. I don't have to wear clothes if I don't want.

Same old Patti, he says, winking at me.

It must be hot in that bird suit, she says. You want to get out of it? We have a hanger around here somewhere. Andrew, where is it? She is on her feet, holding the afghan at her shoulders. She gives Fernando a one-armed hug.

He pulls off his snowy owl outfit and hangs it carefully from the hooks I drove into the bare framing. He is shirtless. The pant part of the suit is cinched around his waist. He drops it, and he too is pretty much naked, wearing only a pair of designer underwear. You don't mind do you? he says, looking down at his skin, which is relaxed and not without its own little handles of flab. Still, compared to me, he is Adonis.

We don't care if you wear anything at all. Do we, Andrew?

What?

I am really never so comfortable as when I'm in my underwear. I do love your house. It's so cool.

Not really, I say. This place is a total disaster.

Don't be such a downer, Andrew, she says. You know you like it here. He does. He's working on the place. We're fixing it up in exchange for rent.

Fernando nods with exaggerated approval, then fishes a monster-size blunt from a hidden pocket in his bird suit.

Same old Fernando, she says.

You got that right.

He lights the joint and we take turns drawing from it.

After a couple hits, he licks his finger and taps it out, and Patti announces that it's time to give Fernando the grand tour.

Oh, please, he says.

She wraps the afghan around her waist, allowing her tits to flop around in everyone's face. I follow as she takes him room to room. Showing off all the dirty brown studs with bent lath nails, the missing sections of flooring and all the plastic-covered furniture, some hers, some mine. And here's the kitchen with its newly mopped ceiling and plywood countertop. That's yesterday's pancake batter. It has turned to glue in the mixing bowl. She throws open the back door and shows off the yard. Mulberry trees have grown through the power lines. The grass is waist high and mixed with thistle and raspberry bramble. The best part is the large concrete tortoise that stands in the middle of it all. I'm not sure how or why it's there, but the snails like it. In the morning, they drag their slimy bodies around its domed shell.

Oh, you have to see Andrew's studio too.

No, I say. It's an embarrassment.

Oh come on, Andrew. Don't be so down on everything.

We climb the steps into my second-floor studio. Clamp lights hang everywhere.

So, he says, this is where the magic happens?

Fuck you, Fernando.

I'm not kidding. I love your work.

My paintings line the walls, stacked together. Most of them are of houses just like this one. It's messed up. It's ruined. I'm building them with color from the foundation on up. It's working here and there.

Really, these are great, Fernando says. You should have totally won one of those grants.

Thanks man, but whatever. I didn't.

Next year, Patti says. Next year he's going to nail it.

Oh man, I'm so hungry, Fernando says.

We head back downstairs. I give the table a quick wipe. We uncap the last of the Colt 45s and dig into the pizza, which we discover is slumped to one side of the box. It's a mess of cheese and sauce. He laughs and then admits to carrying them sideways. I guess it's like a casserole now. We dig out heaps and do our best, eating with only our fingers.

What a gorgeous day, he says as he chews, staring at Patti's tits.

As usual, I am dying of hunger. On my fourth or fifth piece, Patti shoots a look at me.

Slow down big guy, she says.

I stop chewing, suddenly embarrassed by her comment. I look down at my belly, which topples over my pants. I can't even see my own belt. If it weren't for this good pizza, I think I'd walk out of here. This damn stuff is so delicious.

Then Patti starts in on the van. She talks about the hilarious thing with the wheel, and the not so funny cost of fixing it. It's going to fucking break us, she says.

The next thing I know, Fernando is across the room, pulling his wallet from the feathered pocket of his bird suit. He is handing Patti $500 cash. I can't believe this is happening. I am angry and depressed and relieved all at once. I don't have to sell my work for pennies or slave or grovel or anything. I don't know exactly what agreement has been struck. Only I get this strange feeling that I'm the visitor here in my own house.

Patti and Fernando are both laughing and I'm just staring at the bird suit. Feeling heavy, very heavy. I hear myself snort. Wondering how on earth I got here. Why am I the only one wearing pants? Just what the hell is Patti doing.

C'mon, she says, and Fernando stands with her and together they walk into the other room. C'mon Andrew, she says.

Sure, I say, but I can't stand or anything. I'm just stuck here. Stunned. Looking at my huge legs, my big fat belly. Then there is the pizza still in the box and the beer still bubbling in the bottle. It's fucked up that Patti is in the other room right now giggling, making this high warbling sound, butt-fucking naked with her ex, who has just been named one of the eight best artists in Detroit. Fuck them. I guess if something is going to happen between them it's going to happen tonight. I'm not sure I can keep my food down.

I push the table back with my big fat ass. I strip off my pants, pull off my shirt, until I'm naked but for my tighty-whities. My belly is a big hairy barrel. I didn't turn out so great, I know. I am not an award-winning artist either. To top it off, I think I'm losing Patti. I'm planning to insert myself between her and Fernando to stop whatever they are working toward. But the damn bird suit is hanging on the wall, sort of glowing there.

I step into the feathery pants. I can just barely get them around my waist, but the material has a little stretch. It's so very white, with only the faintest pattern, and little flecks of black too. The feathers seem real, each stitched by quill, with a series of complicated knots woven into a fine mesh. I can see there is a real precision and craft to it all. I am putting on the top now, slipping my arms into the long wings, and pulling on the mask as well.

I hear them in the other room. It sounds strange and far off. They are still laughing about something. I don't know what could possibly be so funny. I try the wings. They spread a good eight feet, tip to tip. I flap them and feel how they grab the air. I just stirred up a huge cloud of dust.

I waddle into the room.

Oh My God! Fernando shouts. You look so perfect. What a beautiful idea.

Patti has thrown off the afghan and buckles forward with laughter, flattening her tits against her knees. I can see the nice cleft of ass when she bends like that. Fernando has his hand on her shoulder. Now here is a bird to reckon with, he says. Holy shit. That's one big-ass owl. I mean, you look great.

It's OK, I say. I know how I look.

Really great, Patti says. Oh my God! You're killing me.

I waddle away from them, head upstairs and stand in my studio, looking at the painting that I started last week but haven't been able to work on since my rejection letter. I know it's not a bad start. Maybe it'll actually be something. It'll be the one that'll be in all the books, and years from now people will refer to it as a brilliant turning point for me. A new phase.

I step into the bedroom and stand next to our plastic-covered bed under the open roof. With a couple strong beats of my wings, I'm up off my feet. It doesn't take much and I'm rising through the hole, climbing fast, past the basswood tree that towers over the house. It's not as hard as I thought it would be. I can feel the wind coming through the eyeholes. The sky is pink to the west, but fades to blue ahead of me. Darkness is coming. I'm moving into it. I feel small, almost weightless. I'm soaring fast, gliding silently over our street, feeling better than I have in months.

The Perfect Song

That's Me in my best jumpsuit, the same one I'm wearing now with the shining white cape. My legs are apart, my hands on my hips. I am tall and thin and sleek as a fucking cheetah. "Mister Lady Stardust!" it says in big pink script. The bottom of the poster lists my totally legit tour dates. I'm a glittering superhero come to save the Midwest from shitty music. That's what I am.

I paid good money for those sweet posters, and as usual Cass ruined them with her two-ton purse, left them all creased. I flatten them on my thigh, then duct-tape them side by side on the glass doors.

I gotta keep moving. It's not like I'm going to get any help. Cass has already plunked herself down at the bar and is yapping with Roxanne, who I love till the end of time, because no one pours a drink like her, right up to the lip of the glass, every time. So beautiful! But I could really use Cass's shoulders. She is strong as an ox—*a useless ox!* Stronger than me, for sure, but I am stuck hauling in everything: my mixer, speakers, two solid steel turntables, and three heavy-ass crates of records. Meanwhile she sips her pink cocktail. Thanks Cass!

I kick through the doors with the last of my stuff and find Roxanne has her shirt pulled apart and is showing off her tittie, which she recently ruined with a new lame-o tattoo. God! What is that? A grinning skull with thorny vines crawling from its eyes, going willy-nilly all over her rib cage, ending abruptly at her collarbone and dropping as far as her navel. What a sorry shame! It's just such a scourge on her lovely skin. Poor Roxy. Why does she have to be so metal so dark so evil? Glam just is so much, so much, so much better.

Now Roxy, I say. You don't see me pulling out my dick, do you?

Oh, my God, you've got a dick, Roxanne says. Cass, why didn't you tell me he had a dick? Let's see it.

Maybe later. I'm working on my mixer, see.

I'm plugging all these red and white jacks in the right holes, relearning it, as I do every time, this annoying snarl of wires. Then I hoist my speakers up on the tripod stands. They're impossible and I could use a hand, but obviously tattoo talk is more pressing.

After everything is pretty close to done, I sidle up to bar for a celebratory line of coke, and then toss back a shot of whiskey. Roxanne smiles when I slam the empty glass down on the bar.

Ready for blastoff, I head back to my rig and start flipping through my albums when this dude Applejack walks in, and he's like, Whoa! It's the Thin White Duke!

More like The Thin White Dick, Cass says.

Damn, Cass! I'm not talking trash about you.

You will.

NOT!

You will.

I turn to Applejack and say, I'm going to have to divorce her.

Gazing at me in some sort of moment, Roxy says, Did you know Bowie made all his own jumpsuits, even the ones with the stand-up collars and sequins. He did all his own makeup too. Pretty cool, huh? He was always more than just a singer. He was an artist.

I love you Roxy, I say. I'm divorcing Cass and marrying you.

Yeah, Mister Mister Stardust here thinks he invented good music, Cass says. I get to hear about it every day.

That's Mister *Lady* Stardust to you.

Another fact: Since it's my last show before my big tour, there is a buzz about me. That story about me in the paper is going to bring a ton of people out tonight. In fact, more are coming in right now. All these young hipster types with their ironic facial hair and jumbled thrift store style. They are ordering drinks, and Roxy is going to get so busy. Even now, she's moving fast, pouring liquor into tumblers, jamming fruit onto the rims.

Cass gets off her stool and climbs on stage. She is asking me to share my drugs. I slip her the bag and she heads off to the bathroom, her wild head of hair spilling down her shoulders and over the fabric of her shimmery purple top. I think we both know that this shirt looks better on me. Most of her clothes do. I know I don't have knockers to flaunt, but tits aren't everything, man. I mean sometimes a flat chest showing some rib, with a light smoke of hair running happily down the belly and disappearing into the waistband—oh, that's so much sexier.

What's up Mister Lady? It's this hipster dude I know from wherever. He wants to high-five, which is so ridiculous. I intentionally miss his hand, but he tags mine on the downswing. Hey man, he says. I like the Elvis suit.

I shake my head. Bowie, I say. Not Elvis.

Oh whatever. You're spinning the tunes tonight?

I'm about to, yeah.

That really does look like an Elvis thing.

Fuck that.

His comment is totally off base. Stupid kids think they know everything. They don't know shit. For one, Elvis had a high fold in his collar and mine stands on end. Mine is more the uniform of a 70s space traveler. Then I get this momentary vision of my future. Like one day, when I'm old and happily divorced from Cass and stretching heavy at the stomach, I'll iron a fold in my collar, stitch on some rhinestones and try the religious circuit. All for an audience of overweight ladies, the kind that are still full of hope and need, and have miserable husbands, and would come to my hotel so we could unzip each other and lie naked, bosom to bosom, and maybe eat bacon and peanut butter banana sandwiches, right over our naked bellies.

The room starts to fill. There's a blurred din of talk and laughter, which is a good indicator that it's time to rock and roll. I pick up the mic and thank everyone for coming out and announce that we're going to rock, balls out, right now, starting with Supernaut, a B-side called "Lick my Lolly." Yeah, I got the 45 right here. It's a rare treasure. I may be the only one in Detroit with this one, maybe the only one in Michigan. I get it spinning and turn it up real loud.

Man, what a crowd! Their faces have a decent glaze. I'm glad to be their savior tonight—their minister of glitter, their superhero of stardust. I'm committed to pulling the energy out of them and making the whole room hop.

I have the next record cued and ready to go, and across the room I see Cass, talking to Applejack. She's flushed with drugs and seems happy for a change.

As the song plays itself out, I pick up the mic and announce what everyone already knows: I just want to say that I love you all, but this is the last time I'm spinning at this joint. So get your lazy butts off them sticky seats, and get your hips rolling. I got a sweet mix planned for tonight. It's gonna pull your ass cheeks apart and make your muscles move. You got that Applejack?

Right on, brother!

Oh my God, I say, because Roxanne is delivering another drink to me. Somehow she understands my thirst even better than I do.

Does everyone know this album? I say, holding up a copy of *Country Life*. It may have the sexiest cover of all time. Two girls in their itty-bitty, see-through underwear. Damn! Well, I have the pleasure of announcing that these girls are on their way here tonight. They are being delivered by a limo whose inside is lined with cedar boards and a steaming tray of sauna rocks, and they're in there, sweating oils through their skins and sucking on fat red lollypops that turn their mouths to cherry, and wearing this same little underwear. Boys, they're coming! Girls, watch out! The room is about to be very sexy, very soon.

I drop the needle on "The Thrill Of It All," and I'm on a roll. I know I could use a little more blow, but Cass isn't giving up the bag. Mostly I gotta maintain my current buzz and try not to think at all. I gotta use my intuition and move from song to song in a perfect seamless mix, understanding what the muscles in my ass want as well. Because my ass is your ass is their ass is our ass. We are all one great collective ass, waiting to be electrified, to rub and bounce and shake.

Cass is walking up on the stage, and suddenly she wants the mic.

Why? I say. But she yanks it from my hand right as the song is ending, and I'm preparing for disaster.

I hope you're all getting fucked up and having a good time, she says. I just want to remind everyone to tip the bartender, and everybody drink and drink and drink.

She gets a Hell yeah, from Roxanne.

Hell yeah! Applejack gives up another holler.

OK, Cass says, I'm giving the mic back to Mister Mister Ladyfinger. Let's Dance!

I hate it when she takes jabs at my name, but I don't correct her or anything. I just start the record and the whole place vibrates with a warbling synth, then breaks into the big sound of "Fox on the Run."

Everyone's eyes are on Cass as she takes the floor. At least now the hipsters are off their stools too.

It all feels good. Very good, and I spin and spin until finally I need a break, so I put on a long record and step out for a smoke because this new dumb law makes it hard to be a badass at the bar. I got Traffic playing "The Low Spark of High Heeled Boys." I love this song and the sexy idea of kissing cross-dressers with electricity shooting from their shoes.

I've got my back against the brick wall of the bar, just for a minute, trying to align myself with the planets and stars. Way high in the dark sky, the moon is tracking westward. Here I am under its pale light, feeling positive about the night. I'm praying to the heavens and rocket ships above, and to the good pale skin of the moon, that every girl and dude in the bar strip down to their underpants and dance and sweat and celebrate everything human and beautiful.

And then Cass is standing next to me.

How much more do I have on the song? I say. What do you think? Don't ask me.

She tugs the drugs from her bra and shoves a pinch of powder up her nose, then offers the baggie to me. I hit it too, and feel so damn good, and I look at her and smile. The light of the Rally's sign from across the street has gathered in her hair, and everything is nearly perfect; even the street trash, blowing through the gutters, looks natural and good.

I remember a night, years ago, when I pushed her against this very building, and grabbed her hip and gave her a long kiss. It would have made a good photo, my white cape surrounding us, her legs apart, her head tipped back to the moon, her throat exposed to my cool crooked teeth. It would make a good album cover. It makes me miss kissing her, just thinking this. Too bad she won't let me anymore.

When are you going to play my song? she says.

Soon. It just needs to fit in. You know, I can't just play it if it doesn't fit.

Whatever. Don't play it if you don't want to.

I'll play it.

No, I can tell you don't want to.

I can't talk now the song is ending. Soon, though. I'll play it soon, OK?

It's definitely time to pick up the beat. I'm back behind the mixer working it. Then Cass is right there, pulling out her record. Only it's not time. I told her I'm not ready for that. But she is bulldozing her way all over my stuff, and she grabs the mic. I'm not surprised, but it looks like she has taken off her brassiere. Now her purple top is all slack and hanging on the obvious tips of her thundering boobs. She pulls out a piece of paper, and I know what we're in for. She stole it from me—this little thing I wrote. Already I am gritting my teeth, because it was mine to say.

And worse, on the mic, she sounds like a drunk third-grader: This song is about hippies that fuck in the park. This song is about happy cocks going tent to tent, swinging against warm girls whose skin is wild with honey and dripping all down their legs and the perfect summer air, and sweat runs from necks, and all they want is to weave daisies in their hair and grind and grind their hips. Ladies and Gentlemen, this is "*Misty Mountain Hop.*"

Who would have guessed, but it works. She fills the dance floor to capacity, and Applejack is moving the tables to make more room. Cass is hitting it hard. She is delivering herself to the throng, shaking her body, and all her loose waves of flesh, and her wild hair. Led Zeppelin has become a great shaft of light jabbed into the shimmering ass of the night.

I guess I got to hand it to Cass, but I sure hate to do that. Only she has done it, and this is it. We're peaking, I think. The next song is critical. I pull T-Rex from the slipcover and get "Twentieth Century Boy" spinning. It's huge with crunchy guitar. It's almost perfect.

I can't help it. I have to get out there myself. We're all dancing and supremely drunk and finding that very good spot, and we are all sweating and rubbing against one another. I lean back and kick high, and almost slip on a slick of beer but regain my balance, and move right into the beat, and I invert myself, so I am more feeling than I am skin. I forget my body. I become the song. I go inside it and wear it like clothes. And the only thing that might make this song a little better is another drink. I motion to Roxy for a refill but she is already there with her bottle, pouring me full. That's when I notice that once again Cass has removed her top. I can't say why or what inspired her. Only suddenly it feels like we're in some stupid Spring Break video.

Cass! Put the boobs away. I'm yelling it in her ear. Everyone is trying to ignore her but it's impossible. Her tits are brighter than a disco ball. Everything about the night feels ripped apart. There is a rift between me and my people. Cass is rippling and bending the air with her big bad boobs, sucking all the energy from the room right into the bull's-eye of her nipples.

I want to ignore her. I want her just to go away. My record is ending. I'm trying to think. Only the night has hit a major speed bump and has got stuck trying to roll over Cass's chest, one tit at a time. I'm feeling wrong but trying my best to collect myself and plow forward into the next track, but I only have three crates, all just full of used-record-store trash, with no right fix for anything.

Then out of nowhere it comes to me. I realize I gotta quit thinking. I gotta use the lizard part of my brain. I know it's a major shift, but I put on Stooges, "Search and Destroy." I grab my white boa and leap into the air, whirling feathers and cape, and then crash to the floor, but pop right up in front of Cass and her evil boobs, and we're dancing together. Going at it hard. I close my eyes and find the straight driving beat of the drum. It's violent and pure, with a loud crunch of guitar. I get right up against her, forcing her off the floor.

When she grabs me, I go with it. She's got my junk in her hands. It's weird but I'm accepting her grip as part of our dance. I can feel it in the back of my throat. She tugs my zipper hard, from chest to balls, and in a quick, deft motion, she hauls me out. It happens so suddenly. I am feeling the soft wisps of my feather boa glancing against my skin. I'm feeling the air, and all my nerve endings are flicking wild with zing. My dick is alive in her hand. It becomes the head of a Hydra growing and re-growing wild and arching and she is my Hercules come to chop me apart.

You're a drunk slut, she says. She is smiling in her evil way and holding me tight, cock and balls. I can feel my heart beating along with the music, pulsing in her palm with wild aortic pressure. The floor is cleared, except for us, and we move, holding each other, pushing against one another. Cass is smiling and dragging me further from the stage. Here only to cut off my head, not knowing that when she does, two more will grow. And there is only me, and only her, backing up all the way to the video poker machines, stuck in between our love and our hate for each other.

I am sweating rivers and don't care anymore. I'm tired of being dragged around. I finish the job and peel off my jumpsuit and step free, until I am wearing only the air. I have slipped out of my skin. Shed it, so it can grow new. And it's hot in the bar and beautiful as fuck, and my flesh is pale, and my bones are shining and rippling and banded with sweaty bunches of muscle. Mister Lady Stardust,

I am. A cheetah, a leopard, a lion, a minx with heart like a nuke bomb, A-bomb. Napalm! That's right, baby.

The music plays itself out, and I give Cass a long deep kiss, the first in years, and I'm unrolling my tongue right into her throat, right down to her tonsils, and I go further too, past her vocal chords, and stop just before her lungs. Tasting her insides, trying to understand things about our future. Thinking I might taste her bitter words, and know them, and extract them before she can ever say them.

That's when I notice how quiet the bar is. No one has left. They're just staring at me and Cass. But there's nothing to see—just a naked man and a shirtless woman. I scoop up my jumpsuit and head back to the stage. They are clapping for me. It feels like the night is beginning again. I'm half-hard and completely happy. Naked and born again, a baby with brains gone gold and sequined. I am Adam and Eve. I am Alpha and Omega. I am Bowie and T-Rex. I am Iggy. I am sweat and glitter. What does it matter if I ever wear clothes again?

I get behind my turntables. I know just what I'm going to play. It's right on top and ready to go. I flip the record and pick the track. I'm dropping the needle right into the wide groove between songs. The vinyl pops, then crackles. I'm breathing hard. Waiting for the music. Here it comes—the perfect song.

Forest Parker, Poet Laureate of Lumpkin Street

It's still not fair that I had to see the anger management counselor while they let my wife off the hook. Maybe he has some good ideas, but mostly I think he's a dick, leaning back in his chair, flicking his pencil between his fingers. He doesn't care about me, and nothing pisses me off more than listening to him go on about all his tired techniques for *swallowing your pride*. But part of me knows that a small chunk of what he is saying is right. I am wasting my life on anger. I need to be different, entirely different. I was there, sitting in his office on the last day of my sentence, when I told him I'd made up my mind. I was going to change my name and start writing again. He told me that was a little much. Do you want me to change or not? I said.

I tried to make it official last Friday. I filled out the paperwork and stood in line, but it's not as easy as I thought. Well, the government won't let me do it, but I'm doing it anyway. I don't need them. I am Forest Parker from now on. My wife thinks it sounds like a TV name. She knows I'm trying to show everyone that I am someone new, no longer the kind of jerk who might throw a six-pack through the wall and then not apologize or anything, or flip over her favorite plant and just leave the dirt all over the floor and walk away when she tells me to clean it up.

So the thing is, she likes the part of my plan about not being a dick, but when I tell her about how, if I'm going to be famous, I need to start working hard now, she just starts laughing. My wife's job is to make everything seem impossible.

How are you going to be a poet? You don't know anything about poetry. Name one poet.

I'm racking my brain, thinking only of Slayer and all the words that Tom Araya has to memorize for every song. That's a lot of words, and I'm about to brag him up when she says I can't even spell, and aren't poets supposed to know how to spell? That's a difficult comment to digest. She's right, but isn't that like me telling her that she'll never be a good mother because she can't even cook? Everything she makes tastes the same. It's all dry and the noodles get stuck in my throat. But I would never say that.

Instead of starting a fight, I go sit on the porch steps and throw down a beer so cold it burns my throat. When she comes out, I tell her that I think being a poet is more than just putting words on paper, and as far as I know, I'm the only one on Lumpkin Street that's doing it.

She is looking at the house across the street with the plywood screwed over the door and the busted window. Why don't you write a poem about that house, she says.

How do you write a poem about a piece of crap like that? It hurts to even think about it.

All of a sudden, I'm married to the poet laureate of Lumpkin Street, she says, and starts to laugh.

I don't know shit about her laundromat jab. Only I have taken my notebook to the coin laundry on Jos. Campau so many Sunday afternoons, and sat there half the day, and watched her strappy underwear with gauzy triangles of lace get tossed around in the dryer, and thought of all the times I slid them off her legs—not so much anymore.

Poet laundromat, I say. That's a new thing?

Oh my God, it's laureate, dumbass! Look it up, wordsmith!

I pinch my hands over my ears. I don't appreciate her lording over me with her goddamn college degree. I can feel the anger gathering in my blood. I squeeze hard. I keep it in check, and after she shuts up, I go inside and sit down and start to write.

ALL DAY I'M at work slinging paint, and my boss is getting down on me, going after me for drips, like I can't paint. I've been doing it for twenty years, and this fucker, ten years younger than me, is telling me how to do my job, and I get so it's just about all I can do not to knock him off his ladder and slap him in the face with my brush. I'm trying to focus, and keep my shit together, and then at lunch I'm so irritated with him that I leave the guys sitting there on their five-gallon buckets and go to my car and pull out my notebook and write. It feels better, getting it all on paper. And I know I'm on to something good. Something important.

That night I'm sweating because I drank too much at happy hour. I think that's a poet's right, to be a drunk—fuck yeah, it is! But it sets my wife off and she tells me that I'll always be an asshole if I keep drinking, and then she doesn't want anything to do with me and won't talk. I keep telling her that she's wrong, but she keeps ignoring me, and finally she slams the bedroom door and locks me out in the hall. This silent treatment shit hurts, and the pain goes all the way up into my chest and beats like a heart next to my real heart. I bang on the door, but finally I realize that I'm going to smash a hole in it if I stay, so I pull on all my work clothes, get in my car, turn up my Slayer tape, and roar off down the narrow streets. It's so hard not to hit every one of my neighbors' cars. They make a perfect line for smashing into. How many times have they hit mine? Little mysterious scrapes and dents are always showing up on my car, making it look like crap. This neighborhood makes you ugly. If you weren't already when you moved here. It acts on you. It dents you and bashes into you and tears off your mirror and cracks your windows and then invites birds to come and open their assholes and pour long white streaks of shit all over you.

IT'S A WEIRD dumb night at the Motor City Sports Bar, but at least nobody is calling me a fake or a liar. I'm on one of the vinyl stools and I've got my feet on the metal rungs, and I'm working on a poem. I don't care what people think. I'm drinking and writing and feeling somewhat better. And finally, just to get the bland taste of home out of my mouth, I order one of those cevapi sandwiches. There's a young crowd tonight, some regulars, and then some kids that came down from the suburbs to eat the burgers.

By the time I'm on my fourth poem, I'm feeling much better about the world. That's around when Valerie shows up. She puts on the Barry White, and the lights dim, and everything changes, one-eighty. I want to write a poem about that exact moment because it's sort of beautiful. And there is Valerie with her round shoulders and gargantuan eyes! She sits next to me in her tennis-pro outfit with the Appletree logo on her sparkling left breast. She talks and talks and puts her tease on me. I've heard from a friend that she only has to like you just a little to take you home with her. How can I not think of that when she smiles and her eyes light up?

I tell her my name is Forest Parker and I am the Poet Laureate of Lumpkin Street. Valerie gives me a frown and tells me she already knows my name and why am I lying? I clench my teeth and then start to explain the whole thing. She is looking right at my wedding ring, and knowing all these things about me, because this is a small town, and there's only so many of us old-school Polish left here. Then she touches my hand, and sends a shivery zing into my arm and right across my heart. I don't care how annoyed at my wife I am right now, I make a promise to myself. I will not go out to the parking lot with Valerie. I will not! I'm just here to drink and write and sure, I can study her and remember everything about her, so I can write about her later. But I will not walk her out to her car, even if all I need, really need, is to understand just how the inside of her mouth tastes. I will not. It doesn't matter if she is shiny like a fishing lure. I will not leave the bar with her, but I will write a poem to her, in honor of her beauty. That I can do.

I TRY TO sleep but I can feel the resentment coming off my wife like a poison cloud. I can't sleep next to that. I'm still plenty awake so I get up and eat cold pizza from the fridge. Four days old, it's still better than her noodle crap. Then I write and write. I'm thinking about bones and skulls and what makes a body cool. The best part of the skeleton is the rib cage. It's like the fingers of two angry hands coming together. I'm thinking about Valerie's ribs. They're under a smooth layer of skin. There is nothing angry or tense about them. Just soft and pretty—all her parts are like that. I get working on a poem about her and it unfolds just like a flower the very color of her tongue, and it opens in front of me full of the most pungent wild stink. I want to plant my face in this poem. It has turned into something so amazing. I'm shocked by its energy. Only I can't keep it. Even writing it seems like a crime I have committed against my marriage, and I finally tear the whole thing out of my notebook and start over.

THE NEXT DAY is so windy. It's blowing dirt from the driveway and spraying it in my wet paint. I go around the corner to refill my cut can and I get the rim licked off good, and as I'm heading back a huge gust hits my ladder, a tall aluminum thing, and throws it on the ground and puts a permanent bend in it. That's a $200 mistake, but it wasn't my fault. Still the boss is right up in my face for not tying it off, and I'm so pissed I'm shaking, and I know I'm on the edge of fucking up, and that's when I grab him by the neck and am about to hammer him in the jaw. At the last second, I remember the doughy face of my anger counselor, and I let up. But that's it. I'm fired. I go sit in my car, and I can't even start the thing because I'm shaking and just so upset with myself that I'm about to smash into every car in the lot. I sit there a long time just breathing, just listening to the air moving in and out of me. I feel a sour ache wrenching around my gut. It's just because, it actually hurts more not to fight. This shit is real. I know I must feel things more than other people. It's the poet in me. It hurts, God damn it. Today the world is stabbing me in the stomach. One thing is good—at least I didn't do anything that put me in jail.

NOW THAT I have no job, I know I need to work harder than ever on my writing. If I'm going to be famous, this is it. This is like the critical moment of my life. I write every day, right up to the weekend, scrawling my words late into the night, and my wife is sick of the new me and going to bed alone. Then, because I'm tired of getting drunk by myself, I head back to the Motor City Bar. I find Valerie surrounded by a cloud of smoke. Even if she's not feeling like talking, I still sit next to her and sip my whiskey and beer. I pick some songs on the jukebox and write and drink and look over at Valerie. She nods and blows a sloppy cone of smoke into the air, and finally when she feels like talking, I realize how drunk she is. I know right away that she needs help or she is going to end up spread on the floor. She needs to quit drinking. She's one past enough. So I'm doing my good deed for the day and getting my arm around her and helping her through the door. I hold it open with my foot and steady her as she goes. She is talking and slurring on about how

Mexico is so much better than Detroit because everything there is made of the most brilliant color and she could open up the sliding door at this hotel she went to and stand on the balcony and look at the pretty blue ocean with its waves lapping at the beach and rub oils all over her breasts to make sure that she gets a tan but doesn't burn. She is saying this and trying to make slut-eyes at me, but it's not working. She's too far gone, but her arms are powerful, and she wraps them around me and kisses me. I'm just here to help her out. I didn't want to do anything more, and I wasn't mad at my wife or anything. I don't remember exactly how any of the rest happened. I just remember thinking, Oh shit. Oh shit. But she needed help. Later, driving home, I keep thinking that Valerie is like a poem because she is sad and beautiful. She is a poor sweet woman, just throwing her life away at the bar. Throwing herself at one man or another. Her soul is like two glittering water balloons thrown from a rooftop. Flying at my face. Valerie. She splattered all over me.

I'VE NEVER TRIED to sleep in my car before. But I guess this is part of it all. I just know what I did was wrong. I am sorry. I said I'm sorry. I only said it to the air, but I said it. I didn't mean for this to happen, so I'm punishing myself. Valerie is all over me, a delicious soup of her. Later, when I change my mind about punishing myself, I try the backdoor, and realize that my wife has blocked it with a chair. So I drop back into my car and try to make the best of it. Tonight I am surrounded by the sadness of the world. It has pressed its hollow body against mine. Everything will be OK, I tell myself, even though I know it's a lie. Right here on Lumpkin Street in front of my own house, I light a candle and put it on the dashboard. I pull out my notebook and start to write.

THERE'S A PLACE that I went with my wife, years ago, back when she loved me. It was a cinderblock motel on the side of the highway. We were far away from Hamtramck and my jabbering neighbors. We were up north, and everyday we'd go to the party store and buy forties and stick them in the cooler, then hike into the woods, up and over the hills to the sand dunes. The breeze blew through her dark hair, and her smile was so pure and pretty and had nothing in it that curled downward or sneered. We went to this secret beach, where it was absolutely secluded, and we stripped off our clothes and covered ourselves with a blanket and drank all our beer and loved each other like there was nothing else in the world.

That was the furthest I've ever been away from the black static of this city, and also maybe the furthest from all the anger that whirls in me. She fixed me. She grounded me. It was the best thing ever in my whole life, being there with her. We stayed all day, skinny-dipping, maybe seeing only one or two other people the whole time, and not caring if they saw us naked. What did it matter? We are human beings! We were drunk with love and happiness.

I need to go there again, maybe tomorrow. I need to remember what it was that made everything seem so wide open, so possible. I want to try again. I want to be that person who loves so hard it hurts, not hates. It's like my counselor said, I've hated myself into a box.

I wonder what Tom Araya thinks of love. Somehow he must have it worked out. Not me. Look at me, lying across the seats in a car parked in front of my house. A candle lit on the dashboard. I'm keeping a vigil, I guess. I'm going to stay awake for the rest of my life if I have to. I need to get better, and I need to write the best poem, a poem that changes everything, a poem to save my marriage, and maybe even to save me, a poem to make me a name you'll remember forever—Forest Parker, poet laureate of Lumpkin Street, Hamtramck, Michigan 48212.

Wood For Rhonda

I'm already in bed when Rhonda shows up with her annoying tweezers. She works over my chest, plucks away at my gray hairs, dropping them one at a time in a fuzzy little heap on the nightstand.

The gray is a symbol of decay, she says.

I always thought it meant wisdom, I say.

Well, we're getting rid of them. Then I want you to drink your elixir.

We go through this every year around my birthday. She makes me down this terrible concoction. She chops herbs and shreds roots, then crams them into the juicer, which whirls and extracts little dribbles of brown liquid. I gag at the odor. Apparently, it's really good stuff. It's going to change my gray back to brown. It's going to make me a better, tougher, harder man.

Whatever. I'll drink it. I hold my nose and swallow the stuff.

She stands in front of the window, her back to me, and throws out her arms in a sweeping gesture. Look how beautiful the moon is tonight, she says. I can feel it tugging on my blood.

I'm looking too, but it doesn't do much for me. I'm not like that. I'm no witch or wizard or warlock, and have never been especially in touch with my inner-anything. All I feel is tired, I say, and a little sick and groggy from that elixir. I burrow under the quilt, already drifting off. Let's close the shades, I say.

The next morning, I wake, still burping the bad taste of her elixir. I take my antacids and try to go back to sleep. As is often the case before facing the world on Saturday, she opens her legs and tugs me between them. Sex is nice, but sometimes I'd rather sleep. After her failed attempt to rouse me, she heads to the kitchen. I hear her banging around, and doze through most of it. Soon she returns with one of her weird omelets filled with ginseng root and mandrake. Oh God. It smells like something you might scrape from the bottom of a shoe.

Here you go, she says cheerfully. I made you yummy eggs.

I open one eye. Oh, I say, can you put some cheese on it?

No, she says. It'll ruin it. Eat it up. I made it special for your birthday.

I shovel it in, best I can. She waits for me to finish and then comes back to bed. This time when she opens her thighs, I have more to offer. Once I'm inside, she puts a lockdown on me. She holds me there. She bullies my head around, directing my face, my mouth. Slow, slow, she says. Not like that. Too much. Back off. Then we're almost to her big moment of eye-rolling accomplishment, and I lose it. I'm there, right there, but all of a sudden, I'm not.

No! she says, feeling me shrivel. Not yet. Can't you wait? Oh my God! Then in my ear she says these words: Aeque pars ligni curvi ac recti valet igni.

I seem to be experiencing a strange shift in the universe. I'm in some fault line of time and space. I feel my skin pull with a strange tension, my bones meld one to another, my cartilage and tendons tighten too, and all at once my dick is hard as a chunk of pine of spruce of hickory.

Keep it going, she says. I would but everything is so ridiculously stiff. I can no longer thrust my hip, bend my spine, nothing, so she takes the matter into her own hands and finishes the job. She has what she wants. She rolls over exhausted and happy. Amen, she says. I lie there, somewhat stunned, trying to understand what she's done to me. That's a vertical grain running down my torso, and darkened knots of flesh stub from my chest. On top of that, I can barely bend to sit up. What have you done to me?

Uh oh, she says.

Thanks a lot, Rhonda.

I was trying to keep you from losing it.

You did that for sure, but look at me. What the fuck?

At least you can talk.

Over the next several hours, she tries repeatedly to reverse the spell. It's no use. What am I? A strange sanded chunk of lumber with arms, legs, and head. Where is my soft hairy skin? I can barely walk. My joints creak and groan. I refrain from calling her a terrible, no-good witch, but that's what she truly is.

The next day she schedules us a series of appointments. First with a chiropractor who is completely ineffective at un-crinking my crinks, then with a doctor who shrugs and claims he has never encountered anything quite like this; even the ancient shriveled woman at the helm of her coven only shakes her head.

The last guy we see is Rhonda's therapist. He is younger than me but walks with a cane. His knuckles are gnarled to knobs. His skin has an orange cast, but for the life of me I can't see why anyone would wear such a heavy self-tanner.

I've heard an awful lot about you, he says.

All good I hope. I begin to laugh. That's an awkward sound—laughter in a therapist's office.

So, he says, I understand you have had some sexual difficulties?

It's more than that. Look at me. Rhonda turned me into a piece of wood.

That was an accident, she says. You know I just needed my man to be a man.

Of course, hmm, the doctor says. It's not uncommon to have sexual difficulties, particularly in relation to erections. You know, as you get older your sex drive just drops. Especially around your age, how old are you? Fifty?

Yeah, just fifty, but I still like sex.

But you can't do it like you used to?

Before the spell I was good most all the time. So I don't understand why she felt the need to turn me into a chunk of lumber.

I only wanted his little stud to stay studly. I got the spell wrong, and I don't know what exactly I channeled but it was powerful.

Look at me, I say. This is ridiculous.

The doctor nods and scribbles on his pad with awkward jerks of his stiff arm. Then he says, there is a precedent here for testosterone therapy.

Really, I say. What's the precedent?

Oh just some people I've treated in the past with similar unexplainable issues have benefited from this particular therapy.

I nod, but I still don't understand. And what the hell is wrong with this brain shrinker anyway? Why is his skin all stiff and weird looking?

On the ride home, sleet is hitting the windshield in a miserable spray. I ask her, what's up with the doctor? He looks way too young to be hobbling around. Instead of answering she tells me that if I want to meet some new girls and go on a date or something then it's all right with her.

What are you saying?

I mean, maybe it would put some spark back in our relationship.

Are you kidding?

It might help.

I don't even know how I'd start to find a girl that might consider seeing me. For one thing, I'm all stiff and weird. I can hardly sit normal in a chair.

You'd be surprised. Your pecs are so hard. Girls like a dude with hard pecs.

That's because you turned them to wood.

The next day, I start my testosterone therapy. Within hours my skin feels more oily. I'm surprised at how quickly zits crop on my cheeks. I'm not sure if it's softening my fibrous skin or not. Maybe a little. Certainly my sweat stinks with a new nasty tang and my balls begin to hurt too. Those poor things probably haven't done much work over the last several years, but now they have a new senseless fervor.

She says she has a couple leads on a reversal-type spell and needs to drive out to the suburbs to the herb store. Before she goes, she sets the computer down in front of me. Look at this, she says. On the screen is Perfectmate.com. Fill it in, OK. Just for kicks. Just cuz I want you to try. I mean maybe it'll help.

I really don't get it, I say.

Just do it, she says. Do it for me?

I shake my head. I shrug. Alright.

Over the next hour I plug in my information. I'll tell you this, compared to the other bozos using the service, I don't look so bad. Some are even shirtless in their profile pics. I'm surprised to see Ed, my neighbor from across the alley. He's using the service too. There he is with his shirt off. I guess he doesn't look so bad. Maybe it works? For the sake of irony, I remove my shirt and snap a picture. I am a strange, badly chiseled version of a man. I can't imagine anyone will want to date me.

Come to think of it, it's been a while since I hung out with Ed. I decide it's high time I pay him a visit. I hobble out back and pound on his garage door. You in there Ed?

Hold on, he says. He comes limping around the side gate. His skin has an orange cast and grainy texture very much like mine. How could I not notice this before? Hey buddy, he says looking me over, what happened to you?

It's a rare disease you get when you marry Rhonda. I'm turned into a block of wood. I'm fucked up, kind of like you, huh Ed? We're both fucked up. I can barely get around, but I'm supposed to get better. What do you think, will I? It doesn't look like you did.

Oh jeez. You want a beer? Maybe a beer will help. It always helps me.

OK, I'll take a beer.

I sit in Ed's garage, which he's outfitted with a gas heater and all manner of clamps and torches and mechanisms for molding glass tubing. Today he's making a neon sign that simply says Hamburgers. He opens his little fridge and sets two beers on his workbench. This has always been a good spot to pass the time, right here in his shop. He used to only work here part of the week, but since his so-called "factory accident," he doesn't leave the neighborhood much. He explained the details of it months ago, but now I have no reason to believe it was anything but BS.

While we sit there sipping beers, his phone starts ringing. It says Rhonda on the screen. We lock eyes. Then he grabs it.

Ed here, he says. Yeah, hold on. He passes it to me. Your wife, he says, the witch.

I thought I might find you at Ed's, she says.

Yeah, I'm here.

I have one more stop. Then I'm coming home. Do you need anything? she asks.

What I'm thinking is I need some straight answers, but I don't say that. I swallow. I tell her I'm good.

I hang up and look at Ed, who is obviously suffering Rhonda's curse too. Here and there a splinter pokes from his neck. Ok, I say, I guess I'm just stupid. I don't know why it took me so long to put two and two together.

She didn't tell you? I thought you knew. I really thought you knew.

That night as Rhonda and I eat oysters from her favorite seafood store, I ask her the question that's been stirring around in me all day. How many more are there?

How many what?

Men?

Oh, she says, I don't know.

You don't know? That's the most horrifying statement.

Well, it's complicated because of the whole issue with the coven, and I guess if you had come to the meetings like I asked you, you would know that sexual energy is earth energy. It's an important part of being who I am.

That night I receive an email from the dating service. A girl by the name of Cutiepie2 wants to meet me. I can't imagine why. Rhonda urges me to try, just to see. It might give me new energy and help me overcome my current physical setback. I'm not sure how she arrives at the idea that sex with a stranger will help or that Cutiepie2 will be up for it. It doesn't make sense to me, but I allow Rhonda to drive me there under the condition that she wait in the car.

I find Cutiepie2 sitting at the bar with a drink in front of her. She looks even younger and skinnier in person. She sticks out her bony hand and waits for me to shake it. Hers is smooth. Mine is splintery, knobby, and wrong. I apologize for that.

She asks about my cool leather jacket, says her dad has that same one. It's so retro. She likes retro.

Great, I say. I'm old enough to be her dad.

I excuse myself and hobble to the bathroom where I call Rhonda and tell her I'm ready to leave. Save me, I say. She is mad that I didn't even give it a chance. Well maybe I didn't, but I'm ready to go.

I admit this: Rhonda is putting forth a real earnest effort to try and fix me. That night before bed, she serves me the strangest stew of duck eggs, cat claw, and goat tongue. I only wish she would put cheese on it. I can eat just about anything with cheese. Still, I know her intentions are somewhat pure. She is trying to turn me back into the man I was when we first met. I'd like to be that man too.

Finally, she says, she has gotten word from the higher-ups in the state branch of the coven—there is a way to reverse the spell. Supposedly, it's painful. I don't care. I'm up for it. Apparently it involves uttering some phrase in Latin and ramming her palm into my nasal septum. Won't that kill me? Seems like that'll do it.

It's not supposed to, she says. It's just part of the spell. Of course I don't want to hurt you. They say it works, so someone must have already tried it.

No matter what she did with Ed and her therapist and God knows how many more—she may be growing a whole forest of wooden men—she says she loves me the most. I love her too, but I am afraid of her. I'm afraid to be loved any more than I already am.

She sets the table with a white sheet and lights all the candles, which fill the room with a warm glow. She is cloaked in a black, hooded cape. I have never seen this outfit. It's creepy and sexy too. It's impossible not to notice how her breasts rise from the front of her gown. They heave and swell as she breathes. They are round and filled with power. I want more than ever to press against them.

She tells me that it's time to remove my clothes. I have trouble with my pants, but she helps. She tugs them off, folds them, and sets them on a chair. Then she tells me I need to lie flat on the table. It takes some work to get up there, but together we manage.

Then she opens her book of spells and curses. Here I am naked as the day she turned me to wood. She stands alongside me. She gives me one last hug. It's the best hug ever. I feel love all over her. She squeezes me hard. Our cheeks touch and I fumble trying to kiss her. That's enough, she says, and releases me. I have to stay focused.

Ok, I tell her, Let's get this over with.

She places one hand on my heart, another on my dick, and mutters her words: Igni valet recti ac curvi lingi pars aeque. She runs her hand from my chest up to my neck and over my cheek. She grips my face, tilts my chin, and squints, getting the right angle on my nose. She releases her grip on my groin, raises her arm above her head, and clenches her fingers into a hard little knot of bone. It hovers above me. Dark and powerful. She looks intently at my face. I close my eyes, knowing it's going to hurt. It's really going to hurt. I take a breath and hold it.

Bullets For Charlene

Every summer, our parents rent cottages on Black Lake. I'm not planning on going this year, but then Charlene sends me an email saying she dreamed I'd be there, so she's pretty sure I'm coming. I told her I had one about winning the Powerball, so maybe that's on the way too. Well, she's not kidding. She writes back that she also dreamed our mutual friend Anthony would go to jail and that's exactly where he is now. Then remember that lady who lived up the street, Mrs. James? Charlene dreamed about her dead and lying in a casket way before the accident. Mrs. James screwed up on the highway. She lost track of the road and slammed into the back of a flatbed tow truck. Took her head right off. Then Charlene tells me that she dreamed me and her are going to get married. All I can think is that everything she dreams sounds cruddy. It gets me worrying and feeling a little sick, too, about her version of the future.

I look up from my emails. Across the room, Tamera is painting her nails. She's filled the apartment with this vicious chemical stink.

Just to prove it's not true about me and Charlene, I shut my laptop and put the moves on Tamera. First I light our special candle, then refill her wine and pop in the Al Green cassette, the one with her favorite make-out songs. Of course she knows what I'm up to.

You shouldn't have gone out and got drunk without me and then come home and broke the spout off my teapot. Al Green can't fix that.

Superglue can fix it. It's just a teapot.

It was a special teapot. My mother gave it to me. It's from the Netherlands. Each one is handmade. You ruined it.

Instead of having sex, we talk for what seems like forever about my problems, and my inability to treat her things with respect because apparently I'm so self-centered. Then it is too late for screwing because she has an important meeting the next day at work and doesn't want to mess up her morning. Apparently, I am messing her up. So whatever. Now I feel messed up too, and angry, with nothing to do but lie in bed listening to the sound of our neighbors as they argue.

After Tamera turns out the bedroom light, I head back into the other room and write Charlene back that it'll be good to catch up and maybe even get married. Ha Ha.

As I expected, Tamera is pissed about me vacationing without her, but it sure feels good going on my own. Probably just more proof that I am no good. At least I decided to drive up there on my own, even though my fiancé-to-be Charlene offered to pick me up. That would have been pushing it for sure. I like driving solo anyway. It gives me a chance to think and maybe stop for a beer, which I do. I end up pulling into a roadside tavern just outside of Roscommon to watch a chunk of the baseball game, and I don't make it to the lake until late afternoon, just in time for dinner.

It's really good to see everybody, my parents included. Charlene is looking better than I remember. Same old girl, but fuller, rounder in a good way, and her face has softened too. She kisses me right on the lips, just like it's nothing.

Finally, she says, You took forever.

I had a late start, you know.

I'm glad you made it OK. She kisses me again. She does it right in front of everyone. I'm not complaining. It just surprises me, but

I'm alright with surprises. Next thing I know she is putting a beer in my hand.

It doesn't take long before I've hugged all my hellos and we're all settled into lawn chairs and looking out over the lake. Once again, like every year, Dad is drunk and burning hamburgers on the grill. I mean really charring them. I know my mother is trying not to make a big deal out of it because Charlene's parents are there too, but the blackened bricks of meat are not even fit for raccoons. Mom takes the tray of them and dumps them in the trash. Then Dad ends up having to order a pizza, which takes forever because we are so far out. I know my mom is about to kill him, but no one else seems to care. It gives me a chance to do some catch-up drinking and build a minor pre-dinner buzz.

Later, around dusk, me and Charlene drag our lawn chairs and a bundle of firewood down to the private beach. Somewhere across the lake, a couple of yuck yucks are target practicing or whatever, shooting up the country quiet.

I don't remember that from years before, do you?

I don't think so, she says. I don't like it. They're annoying. They're worse than the mosquitoes.

I do remember the skeeters. That's for sure. Not the guns though.

It's a banner year for mosquitoes.

I set up the logs and squirt some starter on them and toss in a match, and the flames climb the wood, crackling and hissing, curling bits of bark as they rise into the air.

Your mom tells me that you have a girlfriend, she says. That true?

Man, all our parents do is talk. They drink that crappy box wine and never stop jabbering.

So do you?

Well, yeah. For eight months.

That's a long time.

Not that long.

Do you love her?

I don't know. How are you supposed to know something like that?

If you don't know, then you don't love her, so I'm not going to feel guilty if I end up kissing you again.

Fair enough.

Even with the heat and smoke rising from the logs, the mosquitoes are a persistent menace. She swats at her arm and flicks off a squashed blot. We sit there for a long while, talking about one thing or another and just staring into the fire, which eventually settles into a decent bed of coals.

The wood must be really dry, she says, it's almost all burned up. Do we have any more?

Nah, just this.

I give it a poke and a fizz of sparks rises fast into the air, high above the trees, turning to ash.

So what's her name, this girlfriend of yours?

Tamera.

Do you call her Tammy?

She hates that.

You ever skinny-dip with Tammy?

No, she's not much of a swimmer.

How do you grow up in Michigan and not learn to swim? Must be something wrong with her.

She's alright. She just doesn't swim.

That doesn't make sense. Let's say you're out there canoeing and you flip over. She's gonna drag you under. She's going to push you right down into the muck trying to save herself, and you'll totally have it coming. Don't say I didn't warn you.

Whatever, Charlene. She doesn't like boats either.

What does she like?

She's not so bad. Lay off, Charlene.

I'm not the one who went and got a girlfriend. How are we supposed to get married if you have a girlfriend?

Do you really think you and me are gonna hitch it up?

Here, she says, and passes me the whiskey. The answer is at the bottom of the bottle.

I take a long drink and stare right into its glass mouth, through the amber liquid and the warped lens, which I aim at the coals of the fire. They are all the way red, and swishing with a slightly drunken blur. They're nice to look at. There's a real heat pulsing in them but nothing that looks like an answer.

I slap a mosquito from her leg and she grabs my hand and holds it there. Hey, she says, Let's you and me go skinny-dipping.

Right now?

Yeah, sure.

Alright. I don't care. Sure.

Oh bullshit, you don't care. Fuck you. Come on.

I take one more slug from the bottle and then follow her through the dark to a grassy spot under the pine trees just a couple feet from the water. I keep thinking of Tamera alone at her apartment, probably watching some movie on the tube, and how irritated she has been about everything lately, doling out her heavy doses of criticism.

We gonna swim or what?

Yeah. OK.

I undo my belt and pull off my shirt. Charlene steps out of her skirt. I'm watching her hands go behind her back and undo her bra. Here we are, all stripped down with nothing between us, not a stitch, only the nice feeling of the warm breeze coming off the water. I'm staring as intently as I can at the shadowy shapes of her body, trying to tighten my focus, because for years I wondered about her and just how she might look in the buff, but now it's too damn dark to make her out, and about all I can tell is that she is, in fact, all grown up.

She takes a step toward me and brushes my knob with the back of her hand.

Oh there you are, she laughs.

I can't believe you just did that.

It doesn't take any more than that little nothing of a touch and I'm pitched in full aching salute. Needing to find feminine shelter. Something warm and smooth to seal around me.

Just as I'm about to suggest we put our clothes back on, Charlene shoves me toward the water.

Better get in quick, she says, before the skeeters bite us in all the good spots.

We cross the sandy beach, over the slimy bottom and past rocks into waist-deep water. I'm counting on its coolness to shrink me, but the lake feels pretty damn fabulous. We dive in and paddle around each other, making our way through a creepy patch of weeds until we can no longer touch the bottom.

I'm glad you came, she said. I thought I was going to be sitting around the cabin all weekend with Mom and Dad.

Me too, I say. It's great here, and it's real good to see you.

We are treading water, just feet apart. I can feel the little currents she is stirring up with her legs. Above us, the sky stretches forever with all its unfathomable depth, galaxies, black holes, nebulae, and zillions of stars. Looks like the northern lights might be starting too.

When we are fully puckered and mighty thirsty, we work our way back through the shallows, and come out dripping.

Hey, she says, let's dry out on the dock.

I grab my stuff and follow her shadowy body to the end of the rickety structure. She spreads a picnic blanket on the wooden slats.

Let's lie down, she says. That way we can see the stars better.

Seems like a good idea. I start to get on my underwear but she stops me.

We can put towels down and cover ourselves with the blanket. It's warm enough. We can skinny-stargaze. How about it?

Not without our whiskey.

Well go get it.

Alright. I wrap myself in the towel and head back to the fire pit and grab the half-full bottle. From there, I can't see her at all, only the black of the water, and lights that glint from the far-off cabins. She is completely hidden by the night. I take a swig off the bottle and head back, thinking how good it is to be here, everything about this place, the smell of the air, the lapping sound of the water, and Charlene and whiskey too.

I hand her the bottle and she sits up for the drink.

It's pretty great up north, isn't it?

It always is, she says.

The sky is totally loaded with stars. They are everywhere, and on the far end of the lake the northern lights are stretching upward. Aurora Borealis, man. It's gotten more intense since we quit swimming and now reaches high into the night, shooting long tendrils of reds and greens, fingering the dark with a pale electromagnetic haze.

All the years our families have been coming here, I've never seen it so strong. Must be something wrong with the world to cause such a show, like maybe a nuke went off or another Fukushima leaked its crazy-ass ions into the atmosphere.

It's fucking amazing, I say.

Really nice.

We watch for some time, not saying much, just taking turns swatting the skeeters as they make runs for our blood, sucking at our juices, pulling it all right through the blanket. It doesn't make a bit of a difference. After a good stretch and many sips on the whiskey bottle, she rolls on her side, and turns her face to mine and we kiss.

There, she says, that's proof that you don't love Tammy.

I guess.

Don't bother guessing. It already happened.

I put my arm around her, and she scoots her body against mine, pretty much closing every gap that existed between us, until there is zero distance. Less than zero.

I know this puts a big smudge on Tamera and all our months together. But maybe it's all been wrong anyway. Maybe every kiss with her has actually been some sort of cheat on my future with Charlene. I don't know.

Right then, from the opposite shore, a sudden barrage of gunfire rattles the air. I can feel Charlene tensing up. There is a long moment of quiet. Then a man's voice rises in a garbled rebel yell and trails off into laughter. It's a powerful call for a toast. Then guns again.

I feel like the bullets might just drop out of the night and shower the water around us or smash holes through boards of the deck. I know those little lead slugs don't give a shit about what they hit or whose life they ruin. Maybe they just keep going up, soaring into the sky, past airplanes and satellites. Maybe they make it all the way to the moon and smack its surface with little puffs of gray dust.

Wait, Charlene says, Wait. Don't move. They're going to shoot again. Just wait.

I hold still as I can, listening hard.

God, That Kimchi!

I think Angelo is fermenting. The whiskey doesn't seem to be making it any better.

You should probably hold off on that Korean food tomorrow, I say.

I think you're right, he says.

Angelo, my old friend, in hangdog slouch at the bar, ex-linebacker for a no-win college team, turns to me and says he's missing the good parts of having a wife.

What's that? I ask.

Just, you know, someone to share things with.

That seemed reasonable. I didn't have a wife anymore either, and no one else since my girlfriend called it off. That was shitty because she was better than all right. She was even sort of sweet, but God did we fight. I don't have too many friends, but I do have Angelo, who has money at least, and will not stick a knife in your back like some friends, but it's true, his company comes with a malodorous price.

We clink glasses and as we drink, somewhere inside him a seal breaks and a dirty sputter blurts from his meaty buttocks. Oh, he says, oh jeez, oh man, I truly apologize for that.

I finish my drink and call for the tab. People are making faces at us, curling their lips. It's late, and yes we are drunk and smelly. To make it worse, I'm right at the edge of the spins, despite my earlier promise to myself that I'd take it easy.

Out on the curb, trying for a taxi, Angelo stands in his own special cloud. It's followed him here, halfway around the world. The cars whiz by, smartly ignoring us.

Finally, one pulls over, and we're in and moving fast.

Man, crack your window, I say.

Our taxi careens past neon scribbles of the chintz stores on Toy St. That's when Angelo declares we need hookers.

You want hookers? The driver turns around, his eyes wired wide. You need a girl? I know very where to get the very exciting girls.

None for me, I say. Not my thing at all. Not tonight.

Oh absolutely, Angelo says. We need girls. Yes!

The driver makes a couple quick turns and brings the taxi to a stop in front of what looks like an office building and tells us he'll be right back.

Get one without much makeup, I say.

No makeup? The driver says, confused.

Yeah, no makeup, I say.

Don't listen to him, Angelo says. Makeup is fine.

He leaves us there, meter running.

What's wrong with makeup? Angelo says. I like girls with makeup. Just cuz none of your girlfriends ever wore makeup doesn't mean you should punish me.

They didn't need makeup.

Yes, they did.

Would you please roll your window down all the way.

Sorry, he says. I push my fingers over the plastic-covered seat. I close my eyes and try to enjoy being drunk. When I open them, there is a girl between us, leaning into the open door.

This is the guy? she asks. But he's not awake. He's snoring.

Me? I clear my throat. I'm not snoring.

Yeah, you are, Angelo says. You just let out some loud-ass snores, man.

The girl scoots her body against mine. She is heaped with skin, and yes, she wears a thick line of bright lipstick and blue stuff around her eyes too.

Only a minute after the driver pulls away from the curb, she takes me by surprise. Her hand goes right to my leg, up to my groin, and she rubs vigorously.

No, no, no, I say.

You don't want no fun? she says.

I shake my head.

She turns her attention to Angelo, who tells her to wait for the hotel. It's a cozy place, he says. It's got a one-star rating. Our room is a little bigger than this taxi.

Angelo pays the driver. We load up in the lobby elevator. Just before the door closes, a funny smile crosses Angelo's face. He lifts a leg and breaks wind.

Ew, the girl scrunches her face.

Kimchi, he says, shaking his head.

Not good, she says.

OK, thunder-ass, I say, I'm taking the stairs. You two enjoy yourselves. I cross the lobby and throw open a big metal door which slams abruptly behind me and I'm alone but for the buzzing strips of light. Trash litters everything: plastic bags, boxes, Styrofoam cups. The air hangs with the smell of vomit. It's repulsive, far worse than the stench leaking from Angelo's ass. I stand there considering my options, trying not to let the spins take me down. Everything about this place feels wrong. I click open my little stabber, a switch blade from Toy St. and swipe at the air. Don't fuck with me, I say to the dirty room. By the third landing I'm tired of the climb. I stop to rest on a box. I'm barely on it when it collapses and sends me sprawling. I don't hit my head too hard. I don't even care. I lie there, breathing, staring at the underside of the next landing, and the endless tower of stairs above.

When I next open my eyes, Angelo is standing over me with his hooker. I see that she is not wearing anything under her skirt, and is showing a ripe pout of flesh. I take note and decide somebody should advise her of the benefits of underwear. Thankfully Angelo seems to have no trouble scraping me off the floor. It's good to be found. I'm certain he saved me from some terrible kidney-less version of the future.

Finally, I'm in my crappy hotel bunk and faintly sleeping. The air is soured by the odor of sex and the lingering rank of ass. I know the girl is dressing and it takes me a minute to realize—despite her body and nice curve of hip and its obvious similarity to my ex-girlfriend—she has nothing to do with me. I am hoping I still have my wallet, my passport. I don't know. I am already beginning to hurt bad with a brand-new hangover. I've really done it this time. I gotta cut back on the sauce. I resolve to take the next day off drinking. Ha. What a joke! That's when Angelo lets loose a long shuddering blast. I admit there is a certain weird comfort to his flatulence. At least it's familiar. I close my eyes, trying for more sleep. The door is closing. Our hooker is leaving, taking something. I'm not sure what. Just something is gone. What's left is me and Angelo in a swamp of ourselves.

I Don't Feel Sorry For Mrs. Miller

Delivering papers was better in September. That's for sure. Now in November, the wind comes off the Grand Trunk and rushes through this neighborhood just north of Lynch Road, past all those houses with their dingy aluminum siding. It cuts right through my clothes. Sometimes I worry that it will rip the trees from the ground or tear off their limbs and hurl them at me. It takes some getting used to, but after a while I quit worrying and just get my job done.

So far the Millers are my worst customers. I've given them three bills and they've paid nothing, so I'm going to stop their paper tomorrow, but I decide give their door one more try. This time it opens.

I'm collecting, I say.

I see that, Mrs. Miller says. She is clenching her bathrobe together at her neck. Well, c'mon in. It's cold. I get chilly just looking at you.

I'm OK, I say.

How about you sit down for a minute while I find the check-book. I've got some chips and pop if you want.

Nah, I say.

Oh, c'mon. Take a load off. I think Mr. Miller has hidden the checkbook again anyway. Sometimes you wouldn't believe the things he does. She reaches right out the door and grabs the strap of my newspaper bag and tugs it from my shoulder.

The fridge is in there, she says. Go on. Go get yourself a Faygo.

I find a Rock N' Rye and sit down at her table. She takes a seat too and begins writing my check.

That's a big tip, I say.

Well we're late, and I'm sorry, she says. I know you go through a lot to get the papers here. All those early Saturdays while I'm in bed and Mr. Miller is still snoring his terrible snores and there you are delivering papers. Rain or shine. I'm just saying I appreciate it. And anytime you want a break you just knock, OK. I was gone for a long time, but now I'm back and everything is OK again. I'm here most afternoons. Oh, she says, licking her hand. Your hair is sticking up. She rubs down the cowlick on my forehead. That's better.

I CAN HEAR the cars rushing down Lynch Road. They come off the line at Dodge Main and go roaring past the neighborhood on their way to some giant parking lot on the east side. Since it's raining today, they're not gunning it like they usually do. Still, I can hear the water hissing in their new tires. Right at the beginning of my route, I see there is a dim rainbow standing over the houses. It arches between the clouds, landing in the junkyard or the City Airport. The papers aren't always so heavy, but today my bag is crammed full of them, and the cruddy advertising inserts too. The shoulder strap presses a red welt into my collar. Mrs. Miller's place is about halfway through my route. I don't intend to knock or anything but she must have heard me slipping the paper inside her storm door.

You're back, she says. Oh good. I'm so ready for a break. C'mon in. Let's take a break together. Again, she grabs the strap of my bag and hauls me into her house.

There's a rainbow, I say, following her into the kitchen.

Oh really. They happen.

It was right over there. I bet you can still see it from your window. It probably went right over your garage, but I guess it's gone. I stand there for a minute and look at her yard. The garage takes up half of it. Along their chain fence, the Millers have a row of planters made of car tires, set on rims and full of dirt. The flowers in them have given up and gone brown.

Potato chips are in the cabinet, she says. Yeah right there. Will you pour me a glass of wine while you're over there?

Is that you and Mr. Miller in that picture there on your fridge?

Yeah, that's a good one isn't it? We're there at my girlfriend Dorrie's wedding. It was a long time ago, but what a fun night. One of the funnest.

Mr. Miller has a big smile and small teeth that look somehow worn at the edges. Her arm is around his shoulder. Her other hand holds a pink drink in a martini glass. Her hair is so long and wavy, a lot longer than it is now. People are dancing behind them. Glittering decorations hang in the air catching the light.

I have never been to a party like that, I say. All the ones I go to are in basements. Mostly with kids I know from school.

Oh, Mrs. Miller says, do you kiss the girls?

Some parties are like that.

Oh, those must be fun parties, she says.

I don't know. They are OK. I think about those girls, especially Marian and how she let me feel under her bra. She was sweating. Pimples on her shoulders and face. Marian is nice, but she is not as pretty as Mrs. Miller.

IT'S GRAY AND raining again. That makes it hard to keep the papers dry. I flip the canvas flap of the bag over them, but it comes dripping from the rim of my cap, darkening the newsprint. If they get too wet, no one will want to pay, and they'll call the office and complain. I knock on the door. Mrs. Miller is on the phone, but she waves me in and puts her hand over the mouthpiece and tells me to get myself a Faygo. I take off my wet shoes and head into her dim house. There's that snapshot again, the Millers at the party with all that happiness around them. I think they must be drunk. Mr. Miller seems like a short, compact man. Something about his face reminds me of a wolverine, small and tough, baring teeth. I wonder when he gets home every night. I know I'm not doing anything wrong, but I don't think it would be good if he came in and found me sitting at his dinner table. I grab a root beer.

Finally, she hangs up the phone. That was my friend Dorrie, she says. We are planning a revolt. We're both so damn bored.

That's funny.

Dorrie is a funny girl. So tell me what's going on with this flavored lip gloss they sell at all the drugstores. Does your girlfriend wear it? Bonne Bell?

I don't have a girlfriend, I say, which isn't entirely true.

Oh, sure you do. A good-looking boy like you must have a couple at least. So is it weird to kiss a girl that tastes like bubblegum?

All the girls I ever kissed taste more like Hawaiian Punch.

Hah, close enough, she laughs. Well I was thinking of buying some just for kicks. Me and Dorrie were talking about it. I'll get the punch flavor. Then I'll taste just like your girlfriend.

IT'S TRUE THAT no one knows where I go every afternoon. I disappear from the world. If Marian or my friend Donnie came looking for me they'd never find anything. Just the fierce sound of wind rattling around in the bare trees. Mrs. Miller is my secret friend. She smokes her cigarettes and offers them to me too.

You're a natural, she says. That's not your first cigarette, is it?

It is, I say, but everyone in my family smokes. I watch how they do it. I can hold it just like my dad. Like it's nothing at all.

She flips through her checkbook. Again, she doubles my pay. I don't argue. We sit in her living room with shades drawn and the TV playing a movie. Smoke rises straight up from our cigarettes and spreads out across the ceiling. I forget about time, then suddenly realize I'm late. I'm about to put on my jacket when she asks for a hug.

It's been a long fucking week, she says. You don't know the half of it. I can almost not stand it.

Sure, I say.

It doesn't seem weird at all to wrap my arms around her and hold her. She squeezes hard and lets out a little whimper.

For a long minute, we stand together, breathing.

THAT NIGHT I am trying to sleep but I can't. The scent of her hair, her shampoo, the perfume on her neck sticks with me. I keep catching tiny whiffs of her.

THERE IS A dusting of snow on the grass and the sky has a purple knot in it. Mrs. Miller leaves her door cracked open for me, so I let myself in. Hi there, she says from the kitchen table where she sits with a glass of wine. Her shirt is buttoned in only two places and her hair is in curlers. She apologizes for not being presentable, but tells me not to let it bother me.

Are you going somewhere with Mr. Miller tonight?

No, we never go anywhere except the goddamn Moose Lodge so he can get drunk with his friends. No, it's bowling night. I'm in an all-girl league. It's fun. It's a lot of fun. You should meet my friend Dorrie. You would love her.

Really? Why would I love her? Would she like me?

She is so pretty and she tells such funny jokes. You would love her. I love her. You would love her too. She pauses and looks me over. Then says, I'm not sure I want to share you though. C'mere.

She kisses me on the cheek. There, I feel better now. Now go get yourself a pop.

I WALK HOME with a paper bag empty at my side. I smoke the cigarettes that Mrs. Miller gave me. I am not sleeping much at night anymore. I can't. I close my eyes and worry that Mrs. Miller is standing in the dark just outside my room, waiting for me to let her in. She is leaking smoke from her mouth. Through her lips. She wants to weave her fingers together with mine. She wants to suck the smoke from my mouth. I am a hardened smoldering mess. A red ball of fire in the miserable darkness.

I DECIDE TO skip my visit with Mrs. Miller today. I need to feel normal again, but I can't stand not seeing her. I'm making almost no sound as I slip the paper inside her storm door, when she throws it open and pulls me in. She says she has been waiting for me because she needs to know about this skirt. She just bought it from J.C. Penney and needs to decide if she should keep it or not. She spins on her toes to show how it fits. Maybe it's a little snug? What do you think? She lifts her top to show me how it cinches at her stomach. A band of skin puffs over the fabric. I'm not too fat for it, am I?

I don't think so.

Feel it, she says. Right here. She takes my fingers and sticks them under the fabric, right next to her navel. What do you think? she says.

Keep it, I say.

I will.

She walks in the other room and I hear a zipper, then the sound of fabric moving over her skin. She comes back wearing a dress, still unbuttoned in the back. What do you think? she asks. Right then, the sun comes out and it's bright and shines right down the street, even though it's supposed to be doing something horrible like raining ice. She opens her shade to look. For a moment everything is warm and orange. Then it's gone. Isn't it supposed to ice storm? she says.

That's what the weather guy says.

Well nobody told the sun. Button me up, she says. She turns around and I do my best to get the little buttons through the holes. One at a time, I work up her spine, pulling the fabric together at her shoulder blades. She says, this is not the kind of dress you need to wear a bra with, is it?

I don't know.

She turns, holding her arms out from her sides. Well? She gathers her hair and holds it away from her neck. You think I should keep it?

I like it, I say.

This one is definitely better without the bra, don't you think? You wouldn't know it, but at heart I'm a nudist. I'm a closet streaker. I'm a skinny-dipper. Like some days in the summer I can sit around all day with my clothes off. Sometimes in the winter too. I just turn up the heat so it's like a sauna in here and just never put my clothes on.

Dang, I say.

One more dress OK? You'll have to undo me again, OK?

IT WAS SNOWING in the morning, but when I started my route, it turned to sleet and then into rain. By the time I get to Mrs. Miller's, my shoes are soaked through, right into my socks. I knock but she doesn't answer. I try the knob, and stick my head in the door. I'm up here, she shouts from upstairs. C'mon up, and lock the door behind you. The stairs are dark. A faint haze of smoke hovers in the hall. I find her in bed, watching *Jeopardy!* Her dark hair is a wild scribble on her pillow.

I should be downstairs, she says, but I just had the worst night with Mr. Miller and everything still feels wrong. She wipes at the corner of her eyes. I'm just too tired and wrung out to go downstairs today.

It's OK, I say, looking around for a place to sit. The only chair in the room is draped with the dresses she modeled for me the other day. The tags are still attached.

You must be cold. Is it cold out there? If you're cold, you absolutely have to get under the covers and warm up. She pulls the covers back for me and pats the sheets with her hand. I can see the entire side of her body—her shoulder, the flank of her ribs, the heavy skin of her breast, and the round of her hip and thigh down to her knee. The freckles that start at her neck but don't go much past her chest. Compared to Marian, Mrs. Miller's skin is like milk. Poor Marian, with all her zits and moles. I have seen her in a bathing suit and she looks like someone flicked a brush full of paint all over her.

Are you tired too? You look like you might be tired. We could take a nap together if you want. That could be nice.

No, I'm not tired at all. There is not a single sleepy cell in my body. Every bit of me is pitched upward and standing on edge. She tugs on the fabric of my jeans. Why don't you take those off.

I don't know, I say. What about Mr. Miller?

Never mind about him.

I don't understand. How am I supposed to never mind him? He is her husband. This is where he sleeps. That's him in the photo on her dresser, wearing a tuxedo, and that's her in the long white dress with flowers in her hair. I am worried. I don't belong here.

Oh hell, she says. She reaches for my belt and gives it a tug, then goes for my zipper. I know it would feel so good to be in her hand

and wherever else she might want to put me. I stand and back up, out of her reach. Her face clenches with a spasm of disgust. You don't want to, huh?

I start to say something, but I can only shake my head.

Oh Christ, she says. What the hell am I thinking. You're barely shaving.

I shave! I say.

Right, whatever, you're a boy. She throws off the quilt and walks to the bathroom, completely nude. The TV is still playing *Jeopardy!*. The alarm for the Daily Double is going off. She is urinating with the door open, then batting at the toilet paper. I guess I have to take a shower by myself too, she yells. Why don't you at least come here and help me soap up. I look at that photograph of the Millers, newly married, and think how bad it sucks that I'm here in their room, the paperboy with a dumb painful boner. It's fucked up.

Come here, she says.

I can't, I say, I'm not feeling well. I'm going to go.

My stomach clenches. I feel like I'm going to throw up. I am already heading down the stairs. She is swearing and hollering my name. She is telling me to come back.

THE MILLERS HAVE their big colored Christmas lights strung through the bushes on either side of the porch. It has been two weeks now and I have not seen her once. I miss her something terrible. So I knock loud, waiting for an answer, my knuckles hurting with the cold. It's a huge relief when her door opens. I almost step inside but then I realize that it's Mr. Miller standing in front of me.

Is it that time again? he says. How much is the bill?

Oh, um, $5.50.

He flips the checkbook open and frowns at the registry. Either you've been getting some awfully big tips out of my wife, or we're paid up for a good long time. He looks at me, waiting for an answer.

She gives good tips, I say. I can feel the sweat dripping down the side of my ribs.

Teresa, he hollers up the stairs. Come down here. Teresa! The paperboy is here for his tip. I hear her footsteps.

What is it? Her face is slack and more tired than I have ever seen it before. Our paperboy is here collecting. Is this the amount you usually pay? He points to the registry. That's a helluva tip, Teresa.

I'm sorry, I say. You don't have to tip me.

Give me the book, she says.

God damn, Teresa! He slaps the checkbook down on the little table and a stack of mail falls to the floor. He stalks off into the kitchen.

As she's writing the check she leans forward, and in the pale light I can see gray strands of her hair kinked and floating wild above the rest of her. She says, very quietly, that it's too bad the way things turn out sometime.

I want to tell her I miss her, but I'm afraid he'll hear.

You had your chance, she said.

Really? I croak the word.

Really. Her eyes connect to mine. They are narrow and red.

Mr. Miller scuffs his feet against the hall floor and stands there with a beer, shaking his head. Are you going to be ready to go in fifteen minutes? The party starts like now.

I'll be ready, just give me a minute, she snaps.

I take the check and turn from the porch. I hear the storm door squeak open behind me.

Hey, Mr. Miller says. Hey kid! Don't we get a paper?

Sorry, I say, and hand it to him.

He is on the porch in the cold wearing only a T-shirt and jeans, a cigarette burning from his mouth. Thanks man, he says. Sorry about all that.

It's OK, I say.

She is behind him, staring through the door with a face made of stone.

I KEEP THINKING about that photo on their fridge, the smiles on their faces. The streamers. Maybe that's where they are going now. Back to that same party with those same friends and maybe soon they'll be drunk and happy again. I deliver papers to a couple more houses, but can barely get my legs to walk. I just can't see the point of it. At the corner of Eldon and Arcola, I take off the newspaper bag and leave it in the snow. I'm done. When I get home, there is a note from Marian. She wants to know why I'm not calling. I'm not sure what to say to her. I look at it for a long time, but end up dialing the delivery problem line at the newspaper to tell them they can come get their papers if they want. It's a lady I am talking to. She doesn't understand what I am telling her.

I quit, I say. I'm done. And there's this weird pause on the line, and I can hear papers getting moved around.

Can you tell me why? she asks.

I just can't do it anymore.

Hmm, she says. Nobody lasts long on your route. Must be something about that neighborhood. Are you sure there's not another reason?

I'm sure.

Well, that's too bad you're quitting. I'm sorry it didn't work.

Yeah, I say. Well, I'm not sorry. I'm not sorry about a thing.

Ted and His Heartbeat

I landed in Detroit like I land everywhere, like a thrown dog, sprawling, with a huge nervous thump. I filed off the bus, my gear strapped on my back. I didn't call anybody, though I could have. The Greyhound stations usually have a payphone. I decided to hoof it, which seemed like the best way to clear my head. Starting on Woodward I jumped to John R, passed the old Rathskeller, and neighborhood of piled tires and wild rangy trees, empty of houses, to the topless bars and used car shops of Eight Mile, and finally crossed the concrete moat of I-696 into the burbs, back to my own very lame stomping ground. The air is no better in Madison Heights. Nothing is much better, just a lot duller. I'm sorry to say it, but I still hate the place. It's so damn limp, so beige and padded with flab. I mean who says, man, one day I want to live in one of those sweet-ass subdivisions in Madison Heights? I don't know. Maybe my mom did. All I know is I'm allowed to hate it. I grew up here and I've been all over the whole damn country, but there is no place that irks me quite as much.

I made the thirteen-mile trek to Mom's condo, arriving just before dark. It was good to see Mom there at the screen door, even if she was already shaking her head, and didn't seem sure if she should let me in or what.

Jesus, she said. It's about time you come home.

You look good, Mom. She did. She barely had any gray, and only just the faintest beginning of crow's feet at the corners of her eyes. We hugged and she remarked about me needing a shower.

She was right. My skin was sticky. She sent me upstairs, gave me a towel. Showed me the soap, a razor, some shaving cream. I took a while to clean up. The water ran brown down the drain.

I put on my cleanest clothes, which were only just passable. I found Mom in the kitchen smoking a cigarette. She said she was too tired to cook, but she knew I was probably starved, so she ordered a pizza, which is pretty much all I eat anyway, but it's nice to have hot food—way better than eating someone else's discarded leftovers. We sat at the table and she watched me down beer after beer. Not saying anything about how much and how fast I poured it in.

Here I was, after years on the road, knowing I have been such a stupid-ass son. She deserved better, but what she got is me. Her boyfriends weren't much good either.

Is Ted around still? I asked.

Not for a long time. Too bad. I hear he's pretty darn rich now. Married some thirty-year-old tart. I know you didn't like him, but he was OK. He was never mean or anything, and of course without him you wouldn't be sitting here today.

I nodded. I knew that. I was a dick to him. Just like that, I could feel the tears welling up in me. I didn't want to think about it.

After a minute, the doorbell rang. Mom took up her purse and paid the pizza guy.

I didn't realize how starved I was until the food arrived, steam rising from the corners of the box. I folded up a slice of pizza and shoved it in my mouth.

You can stay a while if you want, she said.

Thanks Mom, I said. It seemed like I might, but that wasn't the case. After Mom hit the hay, I went on the computer. I messaged Lotus.

Mom had a bed made up for me, but I didn't feel comfortable in one of those rooms, so I crashed on the couch, underneath one of my old paintings, one of the few that wasn't lost in the fire. Though it showed real potential, I could hardly stand to look at it. Hell. I was only in high school when I made it.

The next morning after Mom left for work, so did I.

I took up my pack and walked another good stretch, dropped south of Eight Mile, and back into the wilds of Detroit. The neighborhood where Lotus lived was not exactly intact. Many of the lots were vacant and tall with weeds or junk trees. Her house was wild too, wild with artwork. It filled me with hope. There were sculptures of both wood and metal rooted in the yard. They climbed right up the side of the house, going all the way to the roof. It was an amazing clutter. I walked up the steps. The door stood open. A cat on the porch, mouth in wide yawn, lazily bared its teeth.

Hey! Hello! Lotus?

I heard a door slam and she came rushing in from the backyard, through the kitchen. There was a broad smile on her face when she hugged me.

Dang it! I never thought I'd see you again, she said.

Yeah. Well. Here I am. Ready to be seen.

She nodded. Yeah. Here you are. Are you hungry? I was gonna make some food. You look like you could use some. You're so skinny.

I could use a beer if you have one.

She opened the fridge and dug a couple cans out of the back.

I couldn't get over how different this girl looked. No makeup or anything. No more piercings. No kinky goth hairdo and black clothes. She was wearing a red shirt, spotted by paint and thumb smears, jeans too, actual work pants. Her hair was cut short and she wore little smarty-pants glasses.

I like your house, I said. It's really cool. What are you? A sculptor now?

Yeah, I got a grad degree and everything. How about you? You still making art?

I met her eyes and smiled and shrugged. I'm drawing is all. Mostly pen and ink. I do a zine too.

That's cool. What's it about?

Roaming the country, jumping trains, dumpster diving, shoplifting, squatting—being a punk. That sort of thing.

You really are a punk, aren't you?

At your service, I said, and opened up my pack and dug around, pulled out a couple issues of my zine, and slapped them on the table.

Oh, this is great, she said, thumbing through it. I recognize your hand still. Can I keep them?

Sure. Hey if you don't mind, I gotta sit down. My legs are rubber. All I've been doing is walking since I got here.

Sure, yeah, see those big pillows over there? Just drag them in here. They're good for chilling. Only I gotta finish cooking. I'm making spaghetti.

OK.

I arranged Lotus's pillows, then slumped into a comfortable heap, flicked the tab on my beer, and listened to the rhythmic chop of her knife on the cutting board. We kept talking even though I couldn't see her face.

I was at my mom's yesterday, I said. First time I'd seen her in years. It was good, but I could hardly stand it. Kept feeling like I was going to collapse into some high-school-jerk version of myself and do something stupid.

You weren't such a jerk. It's not like you burned the house on purpose.

That's true, but I did burn it.

She got out a big pot and filled it with water from the tap, then set it on the stove and cranked up the gas.

Do you remember Ted? He's gone off. I guess he got rich.

We used to rip on him so bad.

Yeah, we did. He was a capitalist is all, but I'm sorry I was such a shit to him.

I slumped a little more into the pillows. I was beginning to relax. Then Lotus delivered me another beer. What about the rest of us? she said. She stood over me for a long minute, just looking at my face.

I'm sorry as hell about all of it.

Me too, she said. I loved the way she looked just at that moment, like she might have some little glimmer of feeling left for me, maybe.

I wanted to ask her if she had a boyfriend. She must. She still had that pitch-black hair that's so nice, and such fine features. Her skin was no longer so pale as it was in high school, but held a healthy tan. Her eyes were still wide, unblinking, making it hard not to look at her and drink her in. Yeah, she must have a boyfriend. I remember how Lotus had hated the word "girlfriend," was not going to be anyone's anything. Then I had asked if I could at least call her my friend. Was that Ok? Ehh, she said, just don't call me your anything.

I love it that you're still making stuff, I said. The last piece of decent art I made was lost in the fire.

That was so messed up, she said. She rinsed a couple peppers and chopped them, quickly, efficiently. I guessed there was a lot of these veggies to prep. I was still talking. Drifting on beer a little too. I kept thinking of it all; she was part of it. But I was the one who couldn't handle my shit and had to leave, just disappear, and gouged great big holes in everyone's hearts.

She poured oil in the pan and turned on the burner. Soon the good scent of sizzling garlic filled the room.

It happened on a Tuesday. After school. Remember?

Of course I do. Fucking A! She put down her knife, breathed deeply, but kept her back to me. Life goes on, she said. It just keeps going. I mean for most of us. Then she took up an onion and began cutting again.

Remember, we had taken a shortcut through the subdivision? We went up driveways, along the sides of houses, through backyards.

I was still negotiating my plan to paint her portrait—the final assignment for art class. I had this idea about her posing for me in the buff.

Don't I look good in clothes? she had asked.

I just want to do a nude.

I don't know about that.

My house stood quietly intact. Like the other houses in the subdivision, it was a two-story colonial. Red brick on the first floor, black plastic shutters screwed through the aluminum siding. A place for wasps to mud their nests.

Mom kept the kitchen stocked with snacks. Easy-to-open, single-serving packets; cookies; bags of chips. I liked a glass of milk too. Lotus grimaced when I offered her a pour. She grabbed the cookies and we went up to my room.

We always kissed a lot. I remembered her as a really good kisser. We were so young, but she just naturally knew how to relax and make everything feel so good. I liked doing it in my room. I had a pretty large mirror, and could watch out of one eye. I loved her this way. Tilting her head to mine, the way her jet-black hair spilled down her shoulders, exposing the little feathers that curled from the nape of her neck toward her ears. Her skin was extremely white. A sort of marble tone, like a vampire, a comparison she loved. She bared her canines and hissed and smiled, threatening to suck a hole in my skin.

I know there were all these different factors that contributed to the disaster. I've thought through it hundreds of times. There were so many little things we could have done differently to shift the future. Change everything.

For instance, if she just felt a little more secure about her body and didn't need weed to relax, then I might not have been so lackadaisical about the candles.

If I have to sit still for a long time, she said, I think I need something to smoke.

I understood, but I was all out. We'd already smoked through my stash a week ago.

Shoot, doesn't your mom have a bag?

Somewhere, probably, but I hate digging in her shit.

I know for sure I'd feel more comfortable if we smoked some first. Why don't you check?

Yeah, OK.

My mother's room was not a place I liked to go. It was dark and messy and held the strange, though not so unpleasant scent of her body. Her shades were drawn. Lots of glasses on the nightstand, half-full with water or wine, a pile of clothes spilled from her hamper. She's messier than me. I flipped on the light. I opened the drawers of her nightstand. I checked the medicine cabinet in her bathroom, thumbed through her many prescriptions. I pulled open the storage boxes she kept under her bed. Nothing. Then, I hit her dresser. I worked through sweaters, pants, short skirts, tank tops, exercise clothes—through them all—to her underwear drawer. I ran my hands beneath those little strappy bits of fabric. Some lacy, some silky, even a G-string—a couple of them red, and one black, one white. Dang, Mom! I didn't know how she could wear this shit, bisecting her butt cheeks. Ugh. I just couldn't take thinking of her in these skimpy nothings. Well, in the back of the drawer, I scored weed. I found it in a Ziploc. Next to it was a small pistol, which I had never seen, but it didn't really surprise me. Next to the gun, wrapped in a cloth, not hidden so well, was a thing I wish I had never touched or lifted out, exposing it to air—a rubbery black dildo!

The trouble with my mind was that I couldn't turn it off. I did not want to picture her using this thing—spread, G-string to the side, dildo inside her. I almost threw up. It seemed so sad and lonely and awful. Why couldn't she just have a decent boyfriend? Why would she need to do this? Ted was Ted. He was obviously not doing a good job. Beyond his lack of charm, he probably lacked in other departments as well. Then there was part of me that took responsibility too. I mean, the sheer existence of this thing felt like partly my fault. My real Dad left right after I was born, couldn't handle having kids. He was up and gone after six months of me crying and pooping my pants. He turned up years later at a ski resort in Utah. Then disappeared again. Mom said he had majorly bad issues, like he suffered some mental breakdown. For years we didn't know if he was alive or dead, but then a postcard or something would turn up. I bet he is fine. I know everything would have been better if he just stuck around. Then at least there wouldn't be any Ted and probably no dildos either. I'd be better too.

I returned to my room. Lotus still had all her clothes on, but I did have the weed. I pushed the cluster of candles aside and made room on my desk to roll the joint, then told Lotus about the dildo.

Wow, she said. Your mom is so cool. I want one.

What the fuck? What do you need one for? You've got me.

You're not there in the middle of the night. Like your mom only has Ted some of the time, and think what good that must be. Poor Ted. Why does he have to be so lame?

Seems like each one of her boyfriends is lamer than the last, but this Ted guy is like a big mountain of lameness. I don't know what my mom sees in him. All I know is she met him at a meeting for people who drink too much and want to stop. She's drinking again, but not with him. He is like the color beige. All he cares about is making money.

Me and Lotus passed the joint and listened to a mixed tape she made until I noticed the clock was really ticking. We only had about an hour. I asked if she was ready. Well? Are you gonna do it?

I guess.

Keeping her eye on me, she undid her pants, pushed them down her legs, looped her thumbs into the elastic of her underwear, and off they went too. Then her shirt, and finally she unhitched her bra. She slumped naked on the bed, looking so pale and thin and sort of apologetic.

Don't paint me. I look terrible, she said.

You look beautiful.

Not true.

Yeah it is.

Could you close the shades? The sun is so bright. I don't want to be in the sun. Is it too weird to paint by candle?

I won't be able to see the colors real good. But I could try.

Might be cool.

OK, I said. I pulled the drapes and lit my candles, about ten of them. A couple on the dresser had already leaked big puddles of wax and ruined the finish. Here and there the drapes luffed, letting in brief swathes of light.

I had a canvas gessoed and ready to go. I set it on my small easel. Pinched blobs of paint onto my pallet. About ten colors—but in the dim light coming from the candles, I couldn't really tell the Napthal from the Cadmium or the Ultramarine from the Pthalo. Part of me liked the idea of not knowing.

How do you want me?

Hmm.

Or should I just kiss you and we could forget this whole thing? She leaned forward and put her hand on my knees, then kissed me.

I really do want to paint you. You know that Egon Schiele book you got me.

Yeah. He's so Goth. He's the most Goth of all the Expressionists.

I want to paint you in one of those poses.

I guess.

Sit up, OK? Keep one foot on the floor. Take the other and hold it to your thigh. You can wrap your fingers around your calf. Let your hair fall in front of your shoulders. Down your chest.

I guess it was a nice pose. Only it left her exposed, having her legs apart like that, showing the lippy squiggle between her thighs, which was turned out just slightly because of the angle of her hips and back. It felt bold, not slutty, but like sex was a requirement of her body, and here she was, not asking but insisting.

I admit I kept thinking of Mom and her dildo and her needs, which I couldn't really sympathize with. It just bugged me so much.

How long do we have to do this? Lotus said.

Maybe an hour. Is that too long?

Yeah, that's just about forever. Hey you better shut the door all the way, OK? What if Ted shows up and sticks his head in here.

Oh, he will. Of course he will.

I threw the bolt on the door. Then I started sketching with a pencil, a 5B, not too sharp. I scrawled the shapes, her ovals, her angles, trying to get her scaled right. I found that her body was complicated. It was like nothing else in all the world. The structure was really interesting, I mean, how weirdly shaped are bones? Each one with specific bends and endings, knobbed, knuckled, cupped—and somehow they hold together, and are shaped by the muscles that stretch over them, rippling, bulging, sinking, dipping. Then there's little pads, layers, blankets of fat that add smoothness, and make everything nicer to look at and better to touch. I got going pretty well, slipped into a sort of trancelike state of working. I was totally into it. After I had the basic shapes in place, I mixed the colors, and ran the brush down the canvas, dabbing, smearing. The hour was over in no time at all.

Lotus broke her pose and started kissing me.

Enough of art, she said. Are we going to fuck at least once? I have to get going soon.

I was feeling pretty good about the painting. I thought I could finish it later without looking at her. I had the general idea down.

Good plan, I said. I got out of my clothes, dug up a condom. She flipped on her back, spread herself, and helped me in, and of course it was great, like every time. I slipped down her warm waterslide of skin. Right into the wonderful pool of her body.

It was perfect, but only for a minute.

We heard the car pull up in the drive. She clenched her thighs. Oh God, I think that's Ted. Better check, OK?

Screw Ted. Let's keep going. I plunged onward.

Lotus clenched her legs with a major force of muscle and totally pushed me out.

Come on, Lotus! The door is locked. Who cares about Ted?

You know he bugs me. Just check.

I got up, penis glistening in the candlelight, bouncing around like a weird prehistoric plant. I split the shades, feeling the heat of the candles rising on my chest.

Yeah, it's Ted. He's out there on the phone in his convertible.

Shoot, she said. I think I better go.

Can we finish at least?

She shook her head. I'm sorry. It's not the end of the world.

I can be super quick.

I don't care. It's not going to work. Not with him here.

I wished I could pick up his car and launch it out of the subdivision. Fire it into space. My poor tormented penis was now twitching around, showing off its heartbeat. It didn't help that Lotus was still nude, naked, no clothes on at all. Her lips were so pink and shone with the spit of our kisses. Her chin and neck and tight lines of her arms and small breasts and nipples, which had squeezed down to little points, everything about her was just so beautiful in the candlelight.

Hello, Hello! Ted came hollering his dumb way through the front door. Helloooo! We heard his steps on the stairs. Anyone home? Helloooo!

I didn't answer.

What kind of dumb accent is that? Lotus said.

I think he's from the East Coast. Maybe they all talk like Fozzie Bear out there.

We heard Ted thump into the kitchen, then he slammed the door to the microwave. Probably he was helping himself to my mother's morning leftovers, getting his fix of stale black coffee, probably about to help himself to her cigarettes too, and top it all off with a long, smelly trip to the bathroom, which suffers from lack of fart fan. Like most days, he would probably be at the house through dinner and into the night, maybe even filling a chair in front of the television.

I'm sorry, Lotus said. Tomorrow, OK? We can fuck tomorrow. No one will be home at my house.

Yeah, OK. I guess I can wait.

She flipped on the light and checked out my painting. Not bad, she said.

It had nice deep tones of blue and gray background, and cream for skin, and dark smears rendering her eyes, her navel, soft triangle of her pubes, and pink of her crotch. The angles looked right. The proportions too. Of course, it was not done, but it was a solid start.

She collected her clothes, then poked her head into the hall, and made a quick dash to the bathroom and slammed the door. I listened to the water splash and the batting sound of the toilet paper.

Then he was knocking at my door. Hey Boss, when's Mom getting home?

I don't know.

He held his coffee, had a newspaper folded and stuffed into his armpit, and was now obviously heading for the john. The one in my mom's room was the one he liked. After he closed the door, Lotus came running down the hall on tiptoes. I kissed her one last time, and she socked me in the arm, and told me not to look so glum. Glum, what a word. I was glum. I didn't start the day or even the afternoon feeling so gloomy. But she was right. Nothing felt so good anymore.

She was dressed. She was ready to leave.

That was where I fucked up most majorly. I got dressed and left the room with candles burning, and I remember this brief second when I was aware of the danger, but I didn't care. I didn't really believe it could happen, but somehow, also, I knew it would. I was angry at Ted for a number of things. I was sick thinking about my mother and her needs, and I was irritated that Lotus had called it off. I only wished I could have kept painting. A real painter would not have had to stop. He'd keep going. I guess I was feeling a loud Fuck You welling up in me. My windows were open. The drapes were luffing. The candles were burning, streaming a smoky wax into the air. I turned up the music so Lotus's mix tape was pounding through the walls and floor, hopefully loud enough to irritate Ted.

I followed Lotus to the porch and stood on the slab in my bare feet and watched her go. It's only a half a mile to her house. I remember thinking that I should have walked her, but I wanted to paint some more while my pallet was wet.

I headed into the kitchen for a quick something. I stuck some bread in the toaster and waited. Ted came thundering down the stairs. He sat at the counter in a cloud of his unpleasant breath.

How's the latest art project going?

Oh fine, I said.

I know I should've tried to get along with him, I mean for my mom's sake, but I just couldn't. I just hated the guy.

Are you still cutting down trees and building crappy houses? I said.

I don't know why you have to say it like that. I never built a crappy house in my life. I'm building neighborhoods, Boss. They're good places. Families will live there. He slurped his coffee and took a big wheezing breath.

My toast popped and I smeared it with some peanut butter. Upstairs, my stereo was kicking out the tunes. It beat through the floor. Then it was weird because it cut out with a big sputter of bass, which I guessed to be some glitch in my cassette player. Or I don't know, maybe the amp took a crap, but it was troubling. I slapped my sandwich together. That's when I started smelling smoke.

I remember thinking it was strange that anyone would have a campfire that time of year. For a second, it was a good sort of smell. It reminded me of going off into the woods and sleeping in tents with my mom, and one of her better boyfriends, years ago, and how we roasted apples, cored and filled with cinnamon and brown sugar, all wadded up in tin foil and tossed in the embers.

Hey! Do you smell that? Ted said. What the hell is burning?

That's when I noticed the smoke blowing past the window. I think someone's house is on fire! I headed for the door, Ted on my heels, then turned to look upstairs. Oh God! It was seeping from the small gaps around my door, a curling smoke, terrible and black.

I was quick, two steps at a time, and I threw open my door, not thinking the handle could ever be so hot to take the skin right off my palm. I was met with a storm of bright heat. It blew in my face, a gust of fire. My room was blazing and there was no way to grab anything, not my computer or journal or guitar, but I couldn't let my painting go, because it was still somehow untouched, there in the middle of the room on the easel. I know I was stupid. The flames were so bright. The smoke so black. It climbed right into my throat and singed my hair to little kinks of dust.

I guess something in my head had gone haywire and dizzy. Even though I was choking and burning, I ran in anyway. I seriously fucked up.

It was Ted who hauled me out of there, down the steps, I don't know how. I'm not a light person and he was not in good shape either. But he saved me from becoming a charred fritter of dead nothing.

I remember waking to a strange thumping sound. It was far away, but then closer and closer. I thought I was rising from underwater, coming up for air, for a big breath. I realized the sound was coming

from Ted's heart. It was like every heart I've ever heard but different, because it was his, behind his ribs, his out-of-shape muscle, his
loose skin. He held me and pressed my head against him. He was
swearing. I could hear the words through his skin. We were on the
ground, on the grass out front. He wouldn't let me go. I thought
I could get up, but I just kept coughing. Then I heard him telling
someone to please get him a wet towel for my arms. I knew they
were burned, my cheeks too, my forehead as well.

My mother arrived around the same time as the emergency people
with all their noisy equipment and lights and loud yell of information. I knew the whole thing was my fault. I wish I could've blamed
someone else. But I couldn't. I was the one with the matches and
the stupid candles. All this time I had thought Ted was bad, but I
was the one who really trashed my mom's life. Her whole house,
everything gone.

Please be OK, she said. Please! When I tried to tell her I was
fine, I started coughing and couldn't stop. Ted released me and a
guy in a blue uniform took over. A mask was being pushed over my
mouth. The air was cool and tasted strangely sweet. I was hurt bad
but feeling somehow relaxed. Soon they had my arms draped in
some sort of cool wet gauze.

My mom and Ted had been directed to the other side of the
street and stood among our neighbors. Even the ones who never
come out were there. I guess it was a spectacular show. The heat was
amazing. Ted had both of his arms around my mother. The fire was
snapping the timbers that held up the roof and it was all beginning
to collapse. There we were, this weird nothing of a family, losing
everything.

Suddenly all I had in the world were the clothes on my back. It
was a weird sort of relief. My mom was crying, but she would sur-
vive. I guessed it was time to quit hating Ted. Smudged with smoke,

his clothes a mess, he kept holding her. I closed my eyes and listened to the sound of my own heart. It was beating fast, it was talking about the future. I can hear it still, pushing the blood around my body, throbbing in my ears.

ACKNOWLEDGMENTS

I owe a debt of gratitude to all the writers who have made the trek to Hamtramck to read and potluck and drink beers with me at the Good Tyme Writers Buffet. Thanks to the Knight Foundation, which provided funding for the program. Thanks to all the members of the Public Pool Art Space, whose work helped sustain it. Thanks also to those whose careful readings of my stories helped me write better, especially KD Williams, Maria McLeod, Jessica Frelinghuysen, and Michael Jackman. Thanks to Annie Martin and Wayne State University Press, who worked together to make this book a reality. Thanks to Anne Harrington for giving so much, all and everything. And finally, thanks to the editors of the publications where these stories first appeared. "When Drink, Drugs, and Floor Polish Steal Your Youth and Trash Your Woman" was written for artist Lisa Anne Auerbach's *Tract House* project, and was later published in *A Detroit Anthology* under the title "Stand." "Lucky Fucking Day" appeared in *Fence*. A shorter version of "New Phase" was published in *Nancy Mitchnick: Uncallibrated*. "Part Plant, Part Animal, Part Insect" was first printed in *Stupor*.

ABOUT THE AUTHOR

Steve Hughes is the writer and publisher of Detroit's longest-running zine, *Stupor*, and the collection *Stupor: A Treasury of True Stories*. He is the creator of The Good Tyme Writers Buffet, a literary series that runs out of the Public Pool, a neighborhood art space in Hamtramck. His fiction has appeared in *Fence*, *A Detroit Anthology*, and many smaller, off-the-grid publications. He is the recipient of a 2010 Kresge Literary Fellowship and two grants from Knight Foundation, one in 2013 for his literary series and another in 2015 to fund his work in *Stupor*. Hughes lives in Hamtramck, where he continues to collect stories at local watering holes for forthcoming issues of *Stupor*.